Jake caught her hand and pressed a soft kiss on the back of it.

"No one will bother you. I swear it on my life," he vowed.

Rebecca's wary eyes were focused on the spot where he'd kissed her hand, and then she lifted her eyes to his face, briefly touching on his lips. She moistened hers, and that was all the invitation he needed.

He lowered his head at the same time she lifted her chin, pleased to discover that she needed little prompting. She placed her hands on his chest and softened her lips when he coaxed her response. He asked permission with the tip of his tongue, and as soon as she parted her lips, swept into her sweet mouth.

Blaze

Dear Reader,

I always enjoy writing cowboy heroes, no matter what time period, but here I am again taking a trip back in history. This time it's West Texas, during an era when the presently elite Texas Rangers were accused of questionable conduct.

The hero, Jake Malone, is a present-day Ranger, who readers met when he worked undercover to infiltrate a group of cattle rustlers in *Texas Blaze*. I really liked Jake and couldn't let him slip away without finding him the perfect heroine. Rebecca soon rose from the depths of my imagination to meet the challenge.

And as always, a big thanks to all of you who have allowed me to tell my stories.

Hugs,

Debbi Rawlins

Debbi Rawlins

LONE STAR LOVER

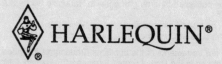

TORONTO • NEW YORK • LONDON
AMSTERDAM • PARIS • SYDNEY • HAMBURG
STOCKHOLM • ATHENS • TOKYO • MILAN • MADRID
PRAGUE • WARSAW • BUDAPEST • AUCKLAND

Recycling programs
for this product may
not exist in your area.

ISBN-13: 978-0-373-79532-1

LONE STAR LOVER

Copyright © 2010 by Debbi Quattrone.

ABOUT THE AUTHOR

Debbi Rawlins lives in central Utah, out in the country, surrounded by woods and deer and wild turkeys. It's quite a change for a city girl, who didn't even know where the state of Utah was until four years ago. Of course, unfamiliarity has never stopped her. Between her junior and senior years of college she spontaneously left her home in Hawaii and bummed around Europe for five weeks by herself. And much to her parents' delight, returned home with only a quarter in her wallet.

Books by Debbi Rawlins

This is for Rena Blake.
You're a terrific lady. I hope you continue
to enjoy reading romances for many
years to come.

1

THE TOWN LOOKED DEAD. Only a few cars were parked along Main Street near Barney's, Appleton's only bar, as Jake Malone pulled his truck to the curb in front of the sheriff's office. Most likely people were sticking close to home still doing holiday things with their families. Jake had stopped by his mother's place on Christmas morning to take her a crystal giraffe to add to her miniature animal collection. She'd thanked him for the unwrapped present, gave him another loud red scarf, and then she'd downed a Bloody Mary while he'd had a cup of coffee, and that had been that. So much for Christmas.

He opened the truck door just as a brisk wind whipped down the center of the street and stung his face. He jammed his Stetson down firmer on his head and then tugged up the collar of his brown bomber jacket, wishing he'd remembered the damn scarf. Out here in West Texas where the wind could cut through a man, he'd have been willing to wear the garish color. Not in Houston, though, where he lived and worked.

Jake spotted Harding's white cruiser alongside the old brick building that housed the sheriff's office. If not for that, he might have thought the place was closed. From the small tinted window, the light inside was dim and neither of the two deputies sat at the metal desk they shared. Normally at this time of the afternoon, the day guy would be pretending to write a report that would end his shift.

But here in this part of West Texas, there wasn't much to report, with the exception of the rustling problem Jake had been called in to help with a few months back. The case had turned out bigger and more complicated than any of them had imagined when Sheriff Harding had first contacted the Texas Rangers looking for someone to work undercover.

Stealing cattle and selling them on the black market had turned out to be the least of the problem. As layers of the case were peeled away and arrests were made, it was clear the rustling was aimed at driving ranchers away from their land. Jake and Sheriff Harding had a pretty good idea who was behind the scheme. They just hadn't proved it yet.

Progress had stalled. Between the court system and the sheriff's slower-than-molasses approach, Jake was losing patience. He didn't blame Harding. He was a decent guy, but too small-town to tackle a case of this magnitude. His deputies were okay, too, but basically a step or two above a rent-a-cop.

Generally that was good enough. Speeding and the occasional DUI were the worst of the crimes the small department faced. Sometimes the local kids got into a bit of trouble, but usually it was just a harmless prank. Nothing more serious than Jake himself had been mixed up with as a teenager, and it hadn't kept him from joining the Rangers. Though he didn't fool himself that his father and grandfather both having been part of the elite group contributed to his being accepted.

He opened the office door, causing the overhead bell to ring, the welcome blast of heat he'd anticipated absent. The place looked deserted. But then he heard Sheriff Harding's familiar shuffle coming from his private office tucked in the corner.

In the next second, the big man appeared at the door, out of uniform, his puzzled frown transforming into an easy smile when he saw Jake. "What are you doing here?"

Jake shrugged. "I was out for a drive and figured I'd stop by to see if there's anything new with the case."

"That's some drive. All the way from Houston." He tossed a newspaper into a wastebasket. "To tell you the truth, this is the first time I've been in the office since last week." He gestured toward a chair near the half-full coffeepot. "That brew's about an hour old. You're welcome to it."

"Where are the other two?" Jake cocked his head toward the deputies' desk before helping himself to a mug.

"Vacation. They're taking turns being on call."

Jake smiled wryly. Things sure were different the farther away from the city he got. He'd grown up in Houston, sometimes working on nearby ranches for extra money during the summer. The experience had helped him with his undercover work as a cowhand at the Double R, and for several months, he'd gotten quite a taste of rural life. At first he'd shaken his head at the laid-back attitudes and lack of sophistication of the folks who herded cows and mended fences. But he'd quickly come to respect their work ethic and dedication to family, something as foreign to him as vacationing on the French Riviera.

"So you got anything for me on Wellsley?" Jake eyed the thick black brew. He favored strong coffee but this looked more like motor oil.

"You best be careful bandying his name about. We don't know for sure that he's behind the rustling. Levi Dodd is the one the courts convicted of organizing the rustling.

Last I heard, he's keeping his trap shut tighter than a bull's ass."

Jake snorted. "West End swooped in to buy every square foot of abandoned land when the ranchers started bailing. Wellsley is not only the company's CEO, but he's a control freak who calls every shot. We both know he was willing to do anything for those mineral rights."

"You're not telling me anything I don't know, but we still haven't tied him to Levi Dodd." Harding shook his head. "You ever do anything besides work?"

"Nope."

"Well, son, us normal folks do." The sheriff rolled a chair away from the desk and lowered his bulk onto the seat cushion. "I know you're not married. Ever been?"

"Nope."

"What did you do for Christmas?"

Jake laughed uneasily. "Why the interrogation?"

Harding shrugged his beefy shoulders. "We only worked together a few months but I like you, Malone. I hate to see you go down the same lonely path so many of our brothers in law enforcement have traveled."

"Hey, better to go alone than drag a family through hell with you." As soon as Jake had spouted off he'd regretted it. He knew Harding hadn't known the illustrious Michael Malone personally, but the sheriff had been around long enough to have heard of Jake's father.

The older man's face softened. "Trust me, son, it doesn't have to be hell. Once you have a family, you tend to shy away from taking so many chances."

Okay, so the sheriff obviously hadn't heard of Jake's father. When it came to the job, a wife and two kids had meant nothing to the veteran Ranger. Until the day he died, the man had known no boundaries. His reckless pursuit of justice had, ironically, been damn near criminal. And in spite of the fact that he'd never had the chance to truly get to know him, Jake admired the hell out of the man. Respect, well, that was a whole different ball game.

He checked his watch. This trip had been for nothing. The case clearly was on hold, and the thing was, he was no longer officially involved, anyway. Not that he was going to back off. "Visited family."

Harding frowned, as if he'd lost the thread of the conversation.

"For Christmas," Jake said. "I visited family." He gulped the last of the lukewarm coffee and stood. He didn't want to be asked any more personal questions. Even if he were inclined to respond, the answers weren't pretty.

He had his mother, who was a functioning drunk, and his older sister, now living in California, who he talked to maybe twice a year. She hadn't married either, or wanted kids, or wanted anything to do with their mother. Blame was big in the Malone family. Lots to go around.

"What are you doing for New Year's Eve tomorrow?" Harding asked, leaning back and rubbing a hand over the top of his thinning brown hair.

"Haven't thought about it yet."

"We're having a small get-together at my house if you're interested in stopping by. There's an extra guest room so you wouldn't have to drive all the way back to Houston."

"Thanks, but I'll be sticking close to home. Maybe I'll go visit our friend Dodd." Jake smiled. "I heard prison isn't agreeing with him. He might be ready to make a deal."

Harding didn't look amused. "Leave it alone, Jake. We'll revisit the case after the holidays."

He lifted his hat, shoved back his hair and reset the Stetson on his head. Past time for a haircut, especially since he wasn't working undercover right now. "I'll check back in a week or two."

"Good." Harding pushed to his feet and followed Jake to the door. "In the meantime, try and enjoy the holidays."

"You, too, Sheriff." Jake tugged up his collar again before stepping onto the sidewalk. No use admitting he'd already seen Dodd. Harding wouldn't like it, and to stay involved, Jake needed the sheriff's blessing.

Dodd had remained uncooperative, but Jake knew he'd riled the shifty little man plenty, gave him a mess of nasty scenarios to think about. A few more days of Dodd looking over his shoulder, stewing over whether Wellsley had decided he was too much of a liability, and maybe Dodd would be more talkative when Jake paid him another visit.

Normally he wasn't one to go behind a man's back. This was Harding's case, but he'd demonstrated that he didn't have the stomach to go after Wellsley. The rustling had been stopped and that was enough for a man like Harding. Not for Jake, though. A lot of ranchers had been hurt and restitution was yet to be made. Besides, Jake had dealt with scumbags like Peter Wellsley before. Rich, powerful men, who thought they were above the law. He wasn't going to get away with it. No matter what it took.

"HEY, HANDSOME, what are you doing around these parts?" Marjorie Meeks stood behind the big oak bar with a towel tossed over her shoulder and her hands on her hips.

The door to Barney's Bar and Grill hadn't even closed behind Jake when the owner's wife had spotted him. He took off his hat and grinned. "I missed you something fierce."

She huffed good-naturedly. "You missed my husband's burgers and grilled onions more than likely."

"That, too." Jake slid onto a stool at the bar, while glancing toward the pool tables. He'd hoped that a couple of the boys he used to play eight-ball with while working undercover would be around. But no luck.

"You just missed Hank and Pete," Marjorie said, bringing out a frosty mug and filling it from the tap with beer. "You won't believe this, but Hank has a date tonight."

"Hank?"

"Yes, sir." She set the draft in front of him and then wiped her hands on her apron. "Never thought I'd see the day that old codger would step out of his dungarees long enough to catch a lady's eye."

Jake nodded his thanks for the beer, and glanced around. The place was empty except for three tables, all occupied by couples, talking, smiling, oblivious to anyone else in the dimly lit room. Apparently Hank wasn't the only who'd be keeping feminine company tonight. Looked like date night in Appleton. The idea depressed Jake. When was the last time he'd taken a lady to dinner, or a movie or even for a drink?

When he'd finally broken his cover, he'd hoped to ask one of the local gals out. Kate Manning was an attractive woman, whose family operated a large ranch not far from town. Like everyone else in the county, she'd known him as one of the Double R hired hands. She'd also suspected him of being a rustler. By the time the real rustlers were caught, and Jake could set the record straight, he'd discovered that Kate was getting married.

Figured. He never seemed to meet decent women anymore. In his line of work, he was surrounded by junkies, the occasional hooker and confidential informants.

"You gonna be wanting a burger? Barney's out back having a smoke but I can get him to—"

"No, don't bother him. I can't stay long. I came to see Sheriff Harding, but I figured I'd drop by to say hey and shoot a game of pool if the guys were around."

She shook her head apologetically. "Christmas week is always slow around here. For ten years I've been telling Barney we ought to close for the week, but he's too stubborn."

Jake smiled and sipped his beer. Funny how at home he felt here, more at home than he did in his own tiny corner of Houston. He lived in a nice enough apartment with all the amenities, but he didn't know his neighbors or even the couple who owned the corner store where he bought beer and bread once a week. Although he had to admit he'd put no effort into socializing.

While living here, as part of his cover he'd hung out with the other ranch hands, did some drinking, shot pool and swapped stories, using the name Brad Jackson. After the guilty parties were arrested, the word quickly spread that Brad was really Jake Malone, Texas Ranger. Some of the guys had gotten their noses bent out of shape because he'd lied to them, but most of the men understood that he'd had a job to do, and were grateful that he'd been instrumental in catching the rustlers.

"You got big plans tomorrow night?" Marjorie asked, while putting some elbow grease into polishing the scarred oak bar.

"Nah." Jake shrugged. "I don't like being on the road with all the amateurs."

She chuckled. "Ain't that the truth. We're going to be open, but nobody who gets liquored up leaves here with car keys. I can promise you that."

Someone had plugged the jukebox and selected a sappy eighties ballad. The love song filled the silence, annoying Jake. He got to his feet.

"Speaking of getting liquored up…" He dug into his pocket and withdrew a few bills that he laid on the bar.

"I don't need to finish this beer. I've got to head back to Houston."

"You sure you don't wanna eat something first?"

"Next time." He set his hat back on his head and slapped the side of the bar. "Say hey to Barney for me."

"He'll be sorry he missed you. So will the rest of the boys. If you change your mind about tomorrow night, a whole group of them are coming around," Marjorie called after him. "You can always bunk at our place till you're ready to drive home."

"Thanks. I'll keep that in mind." He left the warmth of the bar, hunching his shoulders in deference to the cold as he headed toward his truck still parked in front of the sheriff's office two blocks away.

He passed the decorated shop windows that he hadn't noticed the first time…displays of fake snow, Christmas trees and plastic Santas that would be put away in a couple of days.

They made him smile. Funny how he'd taken to the small town. Twice while undercover an eerie feeling of déjà vu had swept over him. The experience had kind of spooked him. Not that he'd ever admit it to a single soul.

At his truck door, he paused and glanced back toward Barney's. Maybe it wasn't such a bad idea to spend New Year's Eve here. He didn't have anything else to do since he'd already turned down invitations from two rangers he worked with. Nice guys but they were married and their parties usually involved other couples, which always made Jake feel like a third wheel.

He didn't have to decide now. Tomorrow he'd see if he felt like company or just sipping a cold beer in front of the TV. He climbed into his truck, popped in a Tim McGraw CD and headed down the highway toward Houston.

One thing he hated about the drive to Appleton was that

for over fifty miles the landscape was boring, with nothing to look at but mesquite and yucca and scrub oak. About twenty minutes away from town, and not having passed a single car, he had to crank up the volume of the CD to help him stay alert. That's why he almost didn't hear the gunning of an engine behind him.

By the time he checked the rearview mirror, the enormous black 4x4 was bearing down on him so fast he thought he'd have to swerve off the road to avoid being hit. At the last minute, the truck swung into the other lane and passed him.

Jake swore loudly, and then watched in amazement as the other truck slowed down, made a U-turn, and headed straight toward him. He applied the brakes and cut to his right. The other driver did the same, but instead of pulling off the road or around Jake, he stopped his truck so that it effectively blocked traffic either way.

Was the guy drunk? Or just plain nuts? Jake saw the driver's door open, and he hesitated before opening his own door, wondering if taking his gun out of the glove box would only make the situation worse. In the next second, he saw the sun glint off a 9mm in the man's hand. He raised the barrel and aimed it at Jake through the windshield.

"No sudden moves, boy. Just get out of your truck nice and slow." Short, heavyset and balding, the man looked familiar.

Jake didn't budge. "You want money, my truck? What?"

"What I want is for you to get out of that damn truck and into mine. *Now*, Malone. I ain't gonna tell you again."

It suddenly registered where he'd seen the man. In court, during Levi Dodd's trial. That meant he either worked for Dodd or Wellsley. Shit. No way in hell was Jake getting into that truck. If he did, he was as good as dead.

"I know you," he said, stalling, while he slowly moved his booted foot off the brake and toward the accelerator.

The man walked closer, leveling the gun, his face flushed. "Put your hands where I can see them and get out of that damn truck."

Jake made his move. He grabbed the steering wheel at the same time he pressed his foot onto the accelerator. The truck shot off the pavement into the brush. The man fired, and the bullet shattered the door window, missing Jake by inches. He ducked from the flying glass, trying to maintain control of the wheel. The truck bucked and dipped over the uneven ground. Two more bullets whizzed past the side of Jake's head.

He couldn't see a damn thing in front of him. What the hell was going on? He blinked, felt something wet on his face. Blood. Shit. He blinked again, saw the big mesquite tree at the last moment and jerked the wheel. The truck rolled once, and then again.

Jake's head hit the top of the cab. He thought he'd rolled again, maybe five times, he wasn't sure. It felt as if he was spinning, being pulled down. Drowning in a sea of dust and wind. His vision blurred and his lids drooped even as he fought to keep his eyes open. He had to get out. Away from the shooter. His gun. He needed to get to his gun. But he couldn't move. Couldn't keep his eyes open. The darkness took over.

THE SUN WAS HOT. Too hot. Yet he was shivering. Jake struggled to turn his face away from the sky. His head throbbed. His lips and throat were so dry they felt blistered. God, he needed water. He tried to get up on his elbows but the pain forced him back down.

Where was he? Why couldn't he…

A flash of memory jolted him. He forced his eyes open.

Managing to peer through slits, he stared at the sharp-needled yucca not five feet away. He was in the desert. But where? How had—? He'd been driving from Appleton. That's right.

His truck. Where was it?

His head and back hurt like a son of a bitch but he forced himself to roll onto his side. He squinted to cut the sun's glare but all he could see was open country. No truck. No highway. Nothing but miles of blue sky, endless stalks of yucca, clumps of cactus and an army of scraggly mesquite.

He tried in vain to moisten his lips. He needed to get out of the sun. Using all his might, he pushed himself up on one elbow. But the pain was too much. He fell back onto the hard ground and surrendered once again to unconsciousness.

2

"REBECCA, stop your woolgathering, girl, and fetch me some more warm water."

Rebecca Swanson blinked, and took a step back from the dark-haired man she'd been so rudely gazing upon. "Yes, Miss Kitty. Right away."

"If I have to tell you one more time to stop calling me Miss Kitty, I'll give you back to them Rangers." The older woman glared, the heavy black kohl around her eyes making her look as fierce as a Comanche warrior.

Rebecca hid a smile as she scurried across the small cramped room to the kettle of water she'd left on the fire. Two weeks ago she would've run and hid had she heard such a threat. But she knew Kitty didn't mean it. She'd been nothing but kind to Rebecca. More than kind, she'd protected her. If not for Kitty, Rebecca was certain she'd be dead.

Kitty wagged a finger at her. "I told you before, I'm not but six years older than you."

It was more like twelve, but Rebecca didn't correct her. Besides, the other whores were always gossiping about one thing or another, in a rather mean-spirited way at times.

Just because they claimed Kitty was thirty-six didn't mean it was so.

Rebecca used a rag to pick up the kettle and carry it to the basin sitting beside the cot. As she poured the water, her gaze went back to the stranger with the long dark hair. Even though his eyes were closed, she knew they were blue. Not a murky greenish-blue like hers, but a darker, more mysterious blue she'd never seen before. He'd opened them twice in the two days he'd been here, but with his fever so high and the amount of blood he'd lost, he'd stayed conscious for only a minute or two.

"Do you think he's going to die?" she asked Kitty.

From her seat beside the stranger, she blinked up at Rebecca in surprise. "No, honey. He's gonna be all right. I wouldn't be wasting my time on a dead man." She looked over at him and wrung out the cloth she used to bathe his wounds. "Even one that handsome."

Rebecca stared down at the man. He *was* handsome, she had to admit, with his square jaw softened by a dimple in his chin, and his perfect mouth. At the direction of her thoughts, her insides clenched. How horrible for her to notice such a thing.

Had she no decency left?

She saw that Kitty was waiting for the fresh dressing, and Rebecca handed her a piece of gauze. "I overheard the doctor say he'd lost a lot of blood."

"It's like that with head wounds. Don't you worry. I've nursed more than my share of men back to health. He'll come around, you'll see." Kitty patted her arm, and then met her eyes, Kitty's green ones darkening with worry. "You've got to eat more, honey. Starving yourself isn't gonna help matters."

Rebecca moved her arm. "I'll get more water."

"I've got enough to worry about. Don't make me fret over you, too."

Rebecca managed a small smile as she reached for the kettle.

"No more warm water. He'll need a cold compress once I'm done." Kitty finished applying the fresh dressing and then got to her feet. "I have to run over to the saloon. You keep the cloth pressed to his forehead."

She nodded, not happy about being left alone with the stranger, though he was in no condition to do her harm. If Kitty had asked her to go to the saloon for her it would have been worse. Rebecca shuddered thinking about those horrible Rangers who leered at her and made awful remarks. She hated those times that she had to be in the same room with them, or had to pass them on her way up the stairs. How very much she wanted to hide a knife in the folds of her skirt, but she'd promised Kitty she wouldn't do that again.

"I won't be long." Kitty threw a wool shawl around her slim shoulders. "He won't cause a fuss. I reckon he'll sleep into the night. When Doc Davis gets back, he'll take over."

Rebecca watched her friend disappear out the door, and then perched on a stool near the wood-burning stove and rubbed the chill from her hands. The cloth had stayed put on the man's forehead so she saw no harm in keeping a small distance away from him. It wasn't that she was afraid. The man was so weak that the scout who'd found him in the desert had had to carry him over his pack mule to town.

He'd had no horse, no hat, and no gun, not even a gun belt. Kitty thought he might be one of those city slickers from back East who couldn't ride worth spit and didn't have enough sense to strap on a gun. She held that belief on account of his fancy boots and store-bought shirt.

Rebecca's gaze drew to the man's bare broad shoulders and upper chest, showing above the sheet that had been draped over him. His skin was tanned and hard, his chest and arms corded with long lean muscle. She didn't have a lot of experience with men, whether they came from the city or not, but she didn't reckon he looked like a greenhorn. She'd helped bathe him some, so she knew his hands weren't soft either, kind of tough and calloused.

She glanced at the well-tooled boots sitting on the floor near the foot of the cot. They didn't look like anything she'd ever seen with the stitching so even and perfect, but then it had been a long while since she'd been around civilized society. It was a shame about his fine shirt. She'd tried to get the blood out, scrubbing so hard that her fingers ached. But the stains barely faded.

Outside, a loud bang came from the direction of the saloon. She jumped up and ran to the window. The noise sounded like a gun. But the Rangers allowed no one but themselves to be armed in town. If someone had broken the rules, it would get ugly out there.

Parting the curtains slightly, she peeked out. Not a soul was on the street. An eerie calm had settled. Rebecca prayed Kitty was all right. For her friend's sake, and for her own.

A man walked out of the saloon, and she immediately released the parted curtains, afraid to call attention to herself. Silly because a person would have to strain to see her, and it certainly wasn't a secret that she'd been helping Kitty here at Doc Davis's place, but living in the shadows had become second nature to her since being brought to the small town.

"Ahh…where…ah—" Behind her the man groaned.

She spun around, her heart racing.

He was trying to push himself up on one elbow. The

cloth that had been swathing his forehead lay on the plank floor, and he'd shoved the sheet down to his waist.

"Don't," she said, rushing toward him, and then abruptly stopped a couple of feet away. "You're hurt. Please, don't try to get up."

He looked up at her, a dazed expression on his face, the pain in his beautiful blue eyes twisting inside her like a knife.

JAKE STARED at the woman with the long blond hair. Who was she? An angel? Was he dead? Pain gripped his head and side, and he sank back, battling the darkness that threatened to claim him again. His eyes closed but he forced them back open. He couldn't be dead. There wouldn't be so much searing pain. His mouth wouldn't be so friggin' dry.

"Water," he whispered, slowly turning back toward the woman.

She stood there, staring at him, her hand pressed to her belly. "Water," she repeated, nodding, while backing away.

He closed his eyes, only briefly, then opened them again to see her standing over him holding a tin cup.

"I'll help you," she said softly, and crouched beside him. She gently slid her hand under his head, paused when he winced, and then slowly lifted his head enough for him to take a sip from the cup.

The cool water felt good on his lips, even better as it trickled down his throat. But the stingy amount she doled out frustrated him. "More," he said, barely recognizing his own voice.

"You have to take it slow." She moved the cup away from his mouth.

With the scant amount of strength he still had left, he grabbed her wrist.

She gasped, and broke free, spilling the water down the front of her dress.

"Sorry," he rasped. "Didn't mean to scare—" He struggled to breathe. "So thirsty."

She turned away, and he thought she might be leaving, but she quickly returned with more water. "You can take only small sips or you'll be sick."

He stared at the front of her blue dress. The outline of her nipples beneath the wet fabric had drawn his attention, but it was the dress itself that startled him. He blinked to clear his bleary vision, which helped little. Although not particularly modest, the dress was odd, kind of old-fashioned.

The woman glanced down and hunched her shoulders. "Where am I?"

She didn't respond right away, but finally said, "Doc Davis's sickroom."

"In Appleton?" At the rough unfinished walls and ancient wood burning stove, he frowned. Even that hurt, and he gritted his teeth. This wasn't Appleton, which was quaint and old, but not to this extent.

"This is Diablo Flats. Do you want more water?"

He nodded, then decided a simple 'yes' would've been less painful.

She inched closer, the slight tremor in her hand making him regret grabbing her earlier. He tried to raise his head but he didn't get far without her help. Again she propped his head while tipping the cup to his lips. He stayed still while she controlled a small stream of water into his mouth. When she withdrew the cup, he didn't argue, though he craved more. She guided his head back down, and then promptly backed away.

He licked his chapped lips. "Where did you say this is?"

"You were supposed to sleep into the night," she said, staring at him with accusing blue-green eyes.

He slowly drew in a breath, pulling the air as deep into his lungs as he could without stoking the fire that raged in his head and along his side. What the hell had happened to him? Why couldn't he remember? He fought against the fog but the only memory he could summon was driving away from Appleton in his truck.

An accident. That had to be what happened. Unaware that he'd closed his eyes, he opened them to see the woman watching him with a mixture of curiosity and fear.

"Thank you," he said. "For helping me."

She blinked, and some of the fear disappeared. "Doc Davis and Kitty have been doing most of the doctoring."

Odd word, he thought, fighting the darkness that beckoned him. The room was strange, too. Cramped, dim, rustic. Maybe he should let go. Fall back to sleep. "How long have I been out?"

Her brows drew together in a slight frown, as if she didn't understand his meaning.

The water had helped, but his mouth was still dry, his voice hoarse. "How long have I been asleep?"

"Almost two days."

"Damn."

She tensed, drawing back.

He tried to smile reassuringly. It hurt like the devil. "May I have more water?"

She glanced toward the door. "Just a little."

He stayed still while she went through the ritual of gently lifting his head and bringing the cup to his lips. After she gave him his ration, she immediately moved away. Then her gaze went to the floor, and sighing, she picked up what appeared to be a rag. She dipped it in a basin of water and then wrung it out.

"We need to keep this across your forehead," she said, hesitating as if she dreaded touching him again. "For the fever."

He gave a small nod, and then closed his eyes, soothed by her featherlike touch. "Thank you," he whispered. "You're an angel." He tried to open his eyes again, but his lids were suddenly too heavy, and the numbing darkness seduced him like the welcoming arms of a lover.

THE DOOR OPENED and a blast of cold air followed Kitty into the small room. "Holy Mother of God, a body could freeze her titties clean off out there." Kitty shuddered, drawing her shawl more tightly around her big bosom. She headed straight for the fire and rubbed her hands together over the dying flame, while glancing over her shoulder at the man. "How's he doing?"

"He woke up." Rebecca laid down the book she'd been reading, and hopped off the stool to gather logs, ashamed that she'd let the fire get so low.

Kitty's eyebrows shot up. "Did he say who he was?"

"No, he seemed confused."

Kitty stepped back to let Rebecca add the pair of logs and stoke the fire. "Was he up for long?"

"A few minutes."

"He still have a fever?"

She was embarrassed to admit she hadn't been checking.

Once he'd fallen back to sleep, she'd moved the stool a fair distance away, planted herself on it, and stared at the rhythmic rise and fall of his chest. In her head she heard his voice over and over again, calling her an angel. If he only knew.

"Rebecca?"

She jumped, and turned to Kitty. "Yes?"

The other woman frowned and moved close enough to flatten her palm against Rebecca's forehead. "You don't have a fever, but you sure are acting peculiar."

"I reckon I'm a bit tired."

Kitty nodded sympathetically. "I'll sit with him awhile. Have you eaten?"

Rebecca glanced guiltily at the two cloth-wrapped biscuits sitting on the dresser. Kitty would fuss if she didn't eat them, so Rebecca picked up the small bundle and unwrapped her long overdue breakfast. She already knew they'd be hard and tasteless but she nibbled at the edges.

"Cook is frying up some chicken for supper," Kitty said, eyeing her. "I'll bring over a piece with a fresh biscuit. I think we still might have a jar of honey, too."

"Don't trouble yourself."

"If your patient wakes up again, maybe we can get a little broth down his gullet."

Her patient? Rebecca followed Kitty's gaze to the man. She wished she had at least asked him his name, but she'd been too flustered to think clearly. "When's Doc Davis getting back?"

The man moaned.

Kitty pulled off her shawl and tossed it onto the coat rack before going to him. "Easy, mister," she said, when he tried to roll onto his side.

He moaned louder, and slowly opened his eyes. He looked straight at Kitty, alarm flaring in his face, and then his gaze went to Rebecca, and he seemed to relax. "Water," he said hoarsely.

Rebecca quickly filled the tin cup and passed it to Kitty, who shook her head. "You go ahead," she said. "He seems to recognize you."

"No, I don't think so."

Kitty gave her a stern look, and helped by lifting the man's head. "Go on."

Rebecca brought the cup to his lips, and he met her eyes while he sipped slowly. Amazingly he seemed stronger than he had just an hour ago. He didn't wait for her to drizzle the water into his mouth, but actually sipped.

"That's enough," Kitty said.

Rebecca moved the cup.

"No. More." His voice seemed stronger, too.

Kitty gave Rebecca a small shake of her head. "Let's wait a few minutes, sugar. You can have another sip, and then we'll get you some broth. How does that sound?"

The man half sighed, half groaned. Kitty guided his head back to the pillow, and he stared grimly up at the ceiling.

"What's your name, sugar?" Kitty asked.

He hesitated, his brows creasing before he said, "Jake. Jake Malone."

"Well, this here is Rebecca. You already know her, and I'm Kitty."

His gaze stopped on Rebecca for an indecently long spell, and she looked away, the heat of embarrassment stinging her cheeks.

The damp cloth slipped off his forehead. Kitty caught it and passed it to Rebecca while she checked his forehead. "Your fever broke."

"Where am I?" His voice was still gravelly but not so weak. "What town?"

"This is Diablo Flats."

"Diablo Flats," he repeated, his face creasing as if trying to puzzle something out. "Right, you said that." He lifted his hand and touched his head where it was bandaged. "I don't remember a town called—" He stopped, his face screwed up as if he'd just recalled something frightful. "My truck. I was in my truck. Was it totaled?"

Kitty and Rebecca exchanged worried looks. "What's a truck?" Kitty asked.

His eyebrow raised in question, and then his gaze slowly slid toward Rebecca. "A truck," he repeated. "You don't know what that is?"

Kitty shook her head. Rebecca just stared.

"You were hurt real bad, Mr. Malone," Kitty said. "A bullet grazed your head, and it looks as though you might've taken a nasty fall. That's why things seem a bit muddled."

He pushed himself up to his elbows, grimacing and moaning with the effort. When it seemed as if he might try to swing his legs to the floor, Kitty got up close and blocked him.

"You best not do that," she said. "You're likely to end up on the floor and I don't expect Rebecca and I would be able to lift you."

"I think I'm okay." Although he sounded stronger than the first time he'd awoken, his breaths came quick and shallow. "I just want to—" He fell back onto the cot.

"Ornery cuss, ain't ya?" Shaking her head, Kitty helped get him settled again. "You haven't had anything to eat in two days, probably longer. You'll need something in your belly before you try to get on your feet. Rebecca, why don't you go tell Cook we could use that broth now?"

Rebecca stiffened, feeling a bit light-headed herself. She'd rather do just about anything than walk through the saloon to the kitchen. Yet how could she refuse Kitty a single thing? The woman had risked a beating to protect Rebecca. Kitty had even talked Doc Davis into letting Rebecca temporarily stay here and help with his patients.

Without a word, Rebecca lifted her shawl off the coat

rack. At least it wasn't dark yet. Most of the men were probably still out patrolling south of town or washing up for supper. Those that bothered to wash, that is. Mainly they were a dirty bunch, both in mind and body.

After sundown it got real bad. The Rangers did most of their drinking then, their whoring and gambling, too. And if the cards didn't go their way, God help everyone because they got downright mean. Lola and Trixie still had bruises from last Saturday night.

Rebecca stopped near the window while she threw the shawl around her shoulders and tried to sneak a peek through the part in the curtains, praying no one was on the street.

"Wait up, honey. I changed my mind." Kitty moved away from the man. "I need to talk to Cook, anyway. He don't need to make that broth too spicy like he does."

Relief flooded Rebecca. She didn't have to look at her friend to know Kitty had probably seen her cowering near the window and was taking pity on her. Rebecca knew she'd have to move back to her room above the saloon at some point. That is, unless she could steal a horse first.

3

JAKE'S HEAD WASN'T POUNDING like it had been earlier, though he was still plenty sore. His stomach growled, and a pang of hunger twisted inside his gut. He wouldn't mind having something more than the broth the redheaded woman had gone after, but he supposed it was best to stay with liquids. Still, it was a good sign that he was interested in eating. Probably an even better sign that he noticed how pretty the blonde was.

She hadn't said a single word to him since her friend had left several minutes ago. Instead, she'd mostly kept her back to him and made a project out of feeding the fire and poking the logs. The tools she used were crude, and he wouldn't be surprised if the wood-burning stove that she faithfully tended was the only source of heat.

He scanned the room the best he could without moving too much and making his head pound again. The rough unfinished walls and the wood plank floors baffled him. The place looked more like a fishing cabin or a line shack than a doctor's office. He could've sworn that's where the woman said he was, but maybe his brain was still foggier than he thought.

He itched to see what was behind him, but straining to

glimpse the antique chest of drawers sitting in the corner and the large tub beside it had fired up the pain in his left temple. Anyway, he'd seen enough. No way this was a doctor's office. The place wasn't even sterile. Jake had to have misunderstood.

"Rebecca?"

She spun around, her hand going to her throat, and regarded him with wide wary eyes.

The swishing sound of her full skirt startled him. He blinked away the sudden fuzziness clouding his vision, and then peered more closely at the old-fashioned dress that was too big for her. If not for the low neckline, the garment looked as if it were something a Quaker or Amish woman might wear. But he didn't know of any religious settlements near Appleton. Besides, not with that neckline... "Your name *is* Rebecca, right?"

She nodded, and closed the stove door, but kept hold of the poker like a weapon. Her hair, tied back at the nape, was so long and thick that it flowed over one shoulder nearly down to her waist.

"Do you live here? Is this your home?"

She moistened her lips, and he noticed the small curved scar near the right corner of her mouth. "For now," she said finally.

"How close are we to Houston?"

She wrinkled her nose. "I don't know."

"Is it an hour from here? Two hours?"

Rebecca glanced toward the door. "Kitty will know."

Jake knew he made her uneasy, but there was nothing he could do but offer verbal reassurance, which he suspected would do no good. Even if he were so inclined, he was in no condition to harm anyone, and she had to know that much. "Were you the one who found me?"

"Goodness no." Her eyebrows went up in surprise, and a small smile tugged at her lips. "Slow Jim found you."

"Slow Jim?"

She nodded gravely. "Good thing he was headed this way or I heard Cook say that the buzzards would've got you." She went to the window and carefully pushed the curtain to the side about an inch, then glanced out before turning back to him. "I expect it's all right to give you more water, if you want some."

"Yes, please."

Studying him with a thoughtful frown, she slowly moved toward a white pitcher sitting on a three-legged stool.

"Is something wrong?"

She blushed. "You have real nice manners, is all," she murmured, and concentrated on pouring some water in a tin cup.

Man, he had to still be asleep and dreaming. The way she spoke and dressed, the roughly made furnishings and the apparent lack of plumbing...

He knew there were folks who lived off-grid, shunning modern conveniences and the use of public utilities, but they'd have to live close to a river or spring, not out here. Except the crazy thing was, he didn't know where "out here" was. But he had to be somewhat close to Houston.

She started toward him with the cup, and he noticed her boots. They were old, worn and laced up the front. She had to be part of some kind of religious sect. The dress was still a mystery though. It wasn't indecent, just not modest enough to appease a religious order.

When she got to his side, she looked uncertain. "Do you think you can raise yourself up a bit?"

"I'd like to try and sit if you'll help me."

She nibbled at her lip. "Miss Kitty might not like that."

"Then she can yell at me."

Rebecca almost smiled as she set the cup next to the basin. "You best be careful. She's not one to take any sass."

"I'll remember that." He winked, and she blushed a pretty pink. "If you give me your arm, I'll try and pull myself up."

"All right, but if you start to hurt—"

"I'm sure it's gonna hurt like a son of a—" He cut himself short, and offered a conciliatory smile. "But I'll feel better sitting up."

She gave a small nod, and faced him, holding out both arms.

Damn, she was small. He had to outweigh her by a good hundred pounds. Fine thing if they both ended up on the floor. He reached up and circled her forearm with his hand. She was small-boned and too thin. At her wrist, where she'd pushed back her sleeve, he saw a scar, as if she'd been bound at some point.

He released her. "I don't want to hurt you," he said. "Maybe we should wait."

She lifted a shoulder. "I'm stronger than I look."

The movement caused the neckline of her dress to slip, exposing the creamy pale skin of her left shoulder. She didn't pull the sleeve back into place, and didn't seem to notice.

He thought for a second that it might be better if she took his hands and pulled him up, but then decided she wouldn't have the strength. At least if he used her arm for leverage he could handle the heavy lifting. Hopefully. He took hold of her arm again, careful not to squeeze too tight. "You tell me if I hurt you, okay?"

She nodded, and braced herself.

Jake slowly lifted his shoulders off the bed and then

paused. With the slight exertion, sweat dampened the back of his neck and the effort hampered his breathing. The pain that stabbed his temple he tried not to think about, but it messed with his vision and he blinked the room back into focus.

"Mister?"

Damn, he wasn't sure he could do this.

"Mister?" She sounded frightened, and her arm started to tremble.

"I'm okay." He breathed in deeply, though it hurt like a mother. "You?"

Her eyes darkened with concern, making them more blue than green. "I don't want you harming yourself further."

"You're the one I'm worried about." He tried to relax his hold on her. "Am I hurting your arm?"

She seemed a bit taken aback, but quickly shook her head.

"Call me Jake, all right? Mister makes me sound old."

One corner of her mouth actually twitched this time, and she shifted, straightening her shoulders, ready to bear more of his weight.

"Okay, I'm ready if you are." It took everything he had to haul himself upright and not curse a blue streak.

Pain shot down his side, and exploded in his skull like a bomb had gone off. Sweat coated his chest and popped out above his upper lip. He swayed to the right, but Rebecca stood firm, cupping her hand over his and steadying him.

"Oh, my, you're awfully pale," she whispered. "Maybe we should lay you back down."

"No." His voice sounded weak. "No," he said again, with more force. "Please."

"All right." She stood as still as a statue, waiting, watching for his cue.

But he had to rest before he made another move. The movement had caused his breathing to labor and each deep pull of air was torturous. He felt as if he'd just run a marathon. Rebecca, on the other hand, hadn't even broken a sweat. She wasn't kidding about being stronger than she looked.

"I might be able to reach the cup," she offered.

"Okay." Water sounded good. Damn good. His mouth was dry and his throat raw from talking.

She stretched toward the table, and fearing he was about to fall backward, he slid an arm around her waist. She gasped, jerked hard to get away, shoving his shoulder.

He howled in pain and fell back.

"I'm sorry." She tried to catch him, but it was too late. "I thought you—I'm so sorry."

He couldn't seem to catch his breath. Tears burned the back of his eyes. He closed them. "Bad idea, huh?"

"Please forgive me." Her voice caught on a sob.

"Hey." He reached out blindly, brushing her arm, and she gingerly touched his hand. "I'll try again later," he said, his voice barely above a whisper. "I need to—I think I'll grab a short nap."

"I'll sit with you," she said softly.

He heard the legs of the chair scrape the wood floor, and then there was blessed darkness once more.

REBECCA WISHED she could remember the words to all of her prayers. But it had been a long time since she'd recited them regularly and she only recalled two for sure. How her mama would be horrified that Rebecca had forgotten something so sacred. She'd be even more sickened if she knew that for a time Rebecca had decided there might not be a God after all. But Mama had long since returned to the earth, and Rebecca suspected she wasn't feeling anything anymore.

After concentrating for a spell, and recalling the order the words were to be said, she murmured the two prayers over and over while she used a cool cloth to bathe Jake's sweaty forehead and throat. This was her fault that he couldn't open his eyes. She should never have shoved him so hard. He hadn't meant to hurt her. He seemed like a nice man. Not like those awful Rangers. He'd even told her to call him Jake.

Jake Malone.

It was a good name, she decided, thinking back to when she was small and living back East. A neighbor boy was named Jake. He'd sometimes pulled her pigtails, but only in fun, and played tag with her and James. The memory of her brother struck a sharp blow. Funny how she should think about Mama and Pa now without crying, but not James. Poor, sweet-faced James.

She used her sleeve to dab at her eyes, and then went back to the task of bathing Jake's face. He'd quit sweating but his chest and shoulders were still damp. She dipped the cloth into the basin, wrung it out and placed it back on his forehead. She hesitated a moment, and then drew the cloth gently down one side of his stubbly face.

He didn't stir, just lay there with his lips slightly parted, his dark lashes resting against his sunburned cheeks. From being exposed to the sun and chill air, his lips had blistered but they were better since Rebecca had applied some cactus sap on them. Kitty had remarked on the swiftness of his healing, but Rebecca had not said a word, for fear her friend, like Doc Davis, would not approve of her medicine.

Thinking of Kitty gave Rebecca a start. How long had she been gone? Most likely she'd found that she had a customer waiting. Rebecca shuddered at the thought. Although Kitty didn't seem to mind, and she took care of business real quick, especially when it came to her regulars.

Rebecca reached for the cloth draped across Jake's forehead, but she didn't pick it up right away. Instead, she stayed quiet and listened to him breathe, first studying the deep dimple in the center of his chin and then watching for movement under his lids. Satisfied that he was truly asleep, she glanced over her shoulder toward the door. Kitty always stomped her boots before entering so Rebecca would have a bit of warning.

Drawing her lower lip between her teeth, she turned back to Jake, and trailed her fingers over his jawline. He didn't move so she boldly traced the outline of his lips, careful of the healing blisters. His skin felt cool so that was a good sign. And if he hadn't tried to sit up, he'd be gaining his strength back all the sooner. Were all men stubborn? She had such little experience. She did know that they were not all this beautiful.

Her gaze went to his flat brown nipples, showing just above where the sheet ended. His skin was smooth, a golden tan color, not white and pasty like some men, or leathery and brown. He had a sprinkling of hair in the valley between his nipples. Not so much to make her nose wrinkle with disgust. Just enough to make her curious about how far down the trail went.

Did she dare look?

Her heart thundered behind her breastbone as she picked up the cloth and dunked it in the water. She wrung it out and then slowly peeled back the sheet to the middle of his flat belly, ridged with muscle. The stream of hair had stopped at his chest and then started again at his navel. Doc Davis hadn't needed to take off Jake's jeans so she could see no farther down. A flash of disappointment shocked her, quickly followed by guilt and shame.

She pulled the sheet back up to the middle of his chest, and then used the cloth to bathe his shoulders. Though she longed to feel the rounded muscle beneath his nipples with her fingertips, she refrained. She kept her spine straight, her hand fisted around the white cloth and concentrated on washing him.

A few minutes later when she heard Kitty on the other side of the door, Rebecca was actually relieved. Too bad he wasn't awake to sip his broth, but she'd heat it later. She returned the cloth to the basin just as the door opened.

She turned to her friend, except it wasn't Kitty. At the sight of the bearded Ranger, Rebecca's insides twisted painfully. She recognized him right off. Corbin. He'd been one of the men who'd rescued her just over two weeks ago. She tried not to cower. She tried not to think about how much she wanted to stick a knife between his ribs.

"Well, looky here, ain't you the good little nursemaid." Mud caked his boots and soiled the plank floor she'd scrubbed this morning. "Why ain't you with the rest of 'em taking customers above the saloon?"

"Doc Davis isn't here," she said, giving him her back so he couldn't see the disgust in her eyes. He'd slapped her once, and if he did it again, she'd have to break her promise to Kitty.

"Do I look sick to you, girl? I don't want Doc Davis."

The floor creaked close behind her. "Look at me when I'm talkin' to you."

Gritting her teeth, she slid a glance at the small bedside table. Nothing there that passed for a weapon. She reckoned she could hit him with the basin if she had to.

"Ya hear me, girl?" He was close enough behind her now that she could smell his fetid body odor, the sour whiskey he'd been drinking. He probably hadn't washed his filthy Levi's or overcoat in weeks.

Slowly she turned to face him, keeping her hands fisted in the folds of her skirt. "Yes?"

"Why ain't you across the street?" He stood but a foot away, the yellow crustiness at the corners of his mouth and around his nostrils making her stomach turn.

"Doc Davis is out making calls. I'm looking after the patient," she said, calm as could be, but hating that her knees had started to wobble.

"Says who?"

"Kitty."

"You take your orders from Wade. Or me. Not that old whore."

"I believe Captain Wade is the one who told Kitty to—"

"You sassin' me?" His bearded face darkened, his blood-shot eyes narrowing to slits as he swayed toward her.

If he touched her...if he even breathed on her once more...

"Rebecca?"

Jake's voice startled her. She spun toward him, accidentally brushing the other man's arm. At the vile touch, she shivered.

"Did you want some water?" she asked Jake.

He lifted a hand to rub his eyes, and then blinked. "Please."

The bearded man snorted. "Please?" He mimicked the word in a high-pitched voice, and then glared down at Jake. "About time you woke up. What the hell were you doing out in the desert with no horse and no gun like you ain't got no sense?"

Jake looked past her and stared at the man, his intense gaze slowly going to the gun belt riding low on

Corbin's hips. She couldn't imagine what was going on in Jake's head. He looked as befuddled as a preacher in a whorehouse.

He shifted, as if he wanted to sit up again. "Are you Slow Jim?"

The other man scoffed. "Shit, no." He wiped his mouth with the back of his sleeve. "I look like a half-breed to you, boy?"

Jake didn't answer, just kept his sights on the other man with what Kitty would call a poker face.

Rebecca quickly poured the water for Jake and carried the cup to him, purposely wedging herself between him and the Ranger. As grateful as she was for the interruption, she didn't like that Jake was lying there weak and defenseless. No telling what might set the Ranger off. Didn't take much when he was drunk.

Jake lifted a hand toward the cup, but Rebecca knew he couldn't drink by himself. She also knew he didn't want to appear weak in front of the other man.

"Let me help you," she whispered, sliding her hand underneath his head.

Behind her, the Ranger barked out an evil laugh. "Hell, looks like you might be good for something other than being a whore, after all."

She stiffened and met Jake's stunned eyes. Disbelief passed like a dark cloud over his features. His gaze roamed her face, searching, growing desperate.

Bile rose in her throat. She swallowed hard, unable to provide him the denial he sought.

4

SILENCE HUNG IN THE ROOM, thick as the smell of burnt bacon. Rebecca lowered her gaze, and Jake concentrated on sipping, trying not to spill the water all over the sheets. Not easy with her hand being none too steady. Rebecca couldn't be a hooker, no matter what that guy said. Hell, he looked like a damn nut case who'd been raiding the Dumpster behind a vintage clothing shop. Except the gun hanging off his hip looked real enough. And he was obviously drunk and spoiling for a fight. Is that why she hadn't rejected his outrageous claim?

As much as Jake wanted to believe that, he couldn't deny the flush of guilt that stained her cheeks or the way she kept her eyes averted. He was good at reading people. It was a big part of his job. Rebecca was hiding something.

"You don't wanna keep your back to me, girly," the man said. "I ain't done talkin' to you."

Jake moved his head, indicating he was done drinking. He'd never been more frustrated in his life, laid up like this, when all he wanted to do was pop the guy in the mouth.

"The thing is," Jake said slowly, wishing he had his gun beside him. "I believe she's done talking to you, buddy."

"No." Rebecca set the cup aside and laid a hand on

his arm. "It's all right." She pulled away and spun toward the other man. "I'm sorry. I was rude to turn away from you."

With the back of his arm, the man shoved her aside and glared at Jake. "Well, now…" His mouth hiked up in an oily smile as he hooked his thumbs into his gun belt. "I ain't one to pick a fight with a cripple but—"

"Just women," Jake cut in.

Rebecca gasped. Out of the corner of his eye, he saw her hand go to her throat. "Please, stop."

The other man swayed but his bloodshot eyes lit with the thrill of the hunt and fixed with intent on Jake.

He used every ounce of strength and adrenaline he had and pushed up to his elbows. He had no friggin' idea what he was going to do from there, but he figured that unless the guy tripped and passed out, it would all be over in a few seconds.

"Stop it!" Rebecca grabbed the man's arm.

"Goddamn little bitch." He tried to shake her off, but she stubbornly clung to him.

"Don't, Rebecca. Stay out of it." Jake grunted with the effort of sitting upright, but he made it, clutching the side of the bed to keep him from going back down.

The door opened and a blast of cold air momentarily broke the tension.

"Kitty!" Rebecca spun toward the door. "Oh, Doc Davis."

A stooped man with white hair, a heavily lined face and wire-rimmed glasses set a big black bag on the floor. He frowned at the tall bearded man, and then at Rebecca's two hands wrapped around his arm.

"What are you doing here, Corbin?" the doctor asked, removing his hat and wearily rubbing the back of his neck. He was a small man, too thin in his oversized brown coat, clearly pushing seventy, but his voice was calm and un-concerned as he faced the taller, stockier man.

"This ain't your business, Doc." Corbin refused to take his menacing gaze off Jake.

"You're standing in my house and smelling worse than a pig in slop, spouting off and upsetting my patient. I'd say that's plenty my business." The doctor hung his hat on the rack, and then shrugged out of his coat. "You can step away from him now, Rebecca. He's leaving."

"Watch it, old man." Corbin jerked his arm out of Rebecca's grasp, and something flashed inside his coat. "You don't want to piss me off."

Jake stared at Corbin. Was that a badge Jake saw pinned to the man's shirt? It almost looked like the star, a Ranger's badge. Jake blinked hard. He was losing it. These people meant well, but he had to get to a hospital.

The doctor chuckled wryly and opened the door. "Get out, Corbin, before any more cold air gets in here and you really get me riled."

Corbin had turned away from Jake and advanced on the doctor. "Who the hell—"

"One more word and the next time you get banged up or shot, don't come to me to patch you up." The older stooped man stood calmly with his hand on the doorknob. He hadn't raised his voice, or moved a muscle, but there was a steely glint in his eyes that said he meant business.

After a tense pause, Corbin muttered a few strong curses as he headed toward the door. "You wait, old man, one of these days it's gonna be you and me."

"If the cold don't get me first," Doc said flatly, and quietly closed the door behind the retreating man. "Holy mother of God," he murmured, waving a hand in the air. "I hope it doesn't take till spring to get the stink out of here."

"I'm sorry, Doc Davis. I couldn't keep him out," Rebecca said.

"Don't fret, child. He's gone now." He walked toward Jake, peering closely. "You look a mite better than when I left yesterday. You sitting up by yourself now?"

Jake half grunted, half moaned. "Yeah, sort of."

"He eat anything yet?" the doctor asked Rebecca, and without warning, used his thumb to pull down Jake's lower eyelid and then bent his head to examine the white of his eye.

"Kitty went to get him some broth."

He switched eyes. "You look good." Nodding in approval, he stepped back. "When was the last time you changed the dressing, Rebecca?"

She told him, and while they went back and forth comparing notes regarding Jake's condition, he studied the man's clothing. He, too, looked as if he hadn't entered the twenty-first century, or the twentieth for that matter. He wore a string tie, suspenders and a homemade shirt. Even his glasses looked old, and a pocket watch was tucked into his vest pocket. It was as if everyone had come in costume.

"His name's Jake," he heard Rebecca say. "Jake Malone, but that's all we know about him."

Her gaze darted between him and the doctor. She still looked flushed and agitated. Either she was still rattled by the incident with Corbin, or the man's words had struck a nerve. Jake sincerely hoped the reason was the former. Although a lot of lowlifes like this guy used the term whore loosely, pretty much pinning the label on a woman who plain wasn't interested.

He clutched the edge of the bed for support, feeling something hard beneath his palm. He looked down, and for the first time realized that it wasn't a bed he'd been lying on but a cot.

"You want to try sitting on a chair?" The doctor moved closer, extending his arm for support. "Rebecca, drag that chair over here, will you, child?"

Jake felt stronger, in spite of the jolting he took trying to sit up. The pain was still there, but his head wasn't so fuzzy any more. He watched Rebecca set the chair beside the cot, her gaze carefully lowered.

"I understand I owe you a debt of gratitude, Doc Davis," Jake said. "You, Rebecca and Kitty."

"It wasn't me taking care of you these past two days. I've been too busy delivering babies and tending a passel of gunshot wounds out past Carter's Creek. Easy there, son."

Jake grimaced as he got to his feet, swaying slightly before lowering his backside onto the hard seat. It wasn't the pain that had thrown him off but rather the remark about gunshot wounds. If this was a religious sect, there would be little to no violence in the community. Nor was this a city where gang activity could result in multiple gunshot wounds.

"You all right?" The doctor peered worriedly at him.

"I'm good." No shirt, but he still had on his jeans, blood-stains and all. "You mentioned treating a lot of gunshot wounds. What's going on?"

Amusement crossed the man's face. "You've got enough of your own troubles, son. The bullet only grazed you, and I reckon your ribs will heal just fine with some rest. The problem was you being without water and losing so much fluid out in the sun. Good thing it's winter. Four months ago and you would've been buzzard food for sure." He took the cup of water from Rebecca and handed it to Jake. "The more fluids you get down your gullet the better."

Jake nodded and drank greedily.

The man turned to Rebecca. "When was the last time you gave him some morphine?"

"It's been a while," she said, ruefully. "I'll get some more."

"Hold on. Only if he needs it. I don't expect another supply to arrive for a month."

Jake nearly choked on the water. "What did you say you gave me?"

"It don't help to get excited." The doctor took the cup from him, pulled out his pocket watch and checked the time. "Morphine is for the pain."

"I know what it is." These people were crazy giving him something that strong. No wonder he'd been groggy and disoriented.

"Is that so?" Doc Davis studied him with new interest. "You must be from back East. Most doctors this far southwest still use laudanum."

"I'm from Houston." And if they came near him with morphine again Rebecca wouldn't think him so well-mannered.

"Houston?" The man's bushy white eyebrows went up. "You don't say."

"How far away are we from the city?"

"The city?" Davis smiled and then thoughtfully pursed his lips. "A couple days' ride on a fresh horse. Now, if you're going by buggy—"

"Wait." Jake held up a hand. "Do you people not use cars at all?"

"I hired a sleeping car when I rode the train to see my sister, if that's your meaning."

"No, I'm talking about a regular car, or a truck." Jake sighed at the perplexed looks on their faces. "Like a four-door sedan."

"Can't say that I heard of any such thing." The doctor frowned, then looked at Rebecca, who shrugged. "Must be something new they started back East."

Frustrated, Jake rubbed his stubbly jaw. Nobody lived that far away from civilization, not in this country. Were they putting him on? They looked serious enough, though, even their confusion seemed genuine. "Cars aren't new," he muttered. "They've been around since the early nineteen hundreds. Maybe even before that. History wasn't exactly my favorite subject in school."

Rebecca looked helplessly at the doctor, who exhaled loudly and scratched his head, appearing far more worried than he should.

An eerie feeling crawled down Jake's spine. "What's going on?"

"Wish I knew how hard you hit your head, son," the doctor said, sympathetically, "but I expect you'll come back to rights before too long. You remembering your name and that you come from Houston is a real good sign."

"I'll take care of you," Rebecca said softly, looking as if she'd given up on him.

"I'm not crazy." Jake's stomach knotted. How could he be sure he wasn't hallucinating? The way these people talked and dressed. There was too much detail for this to be a dream.

"We're not saying you are. Just confused." The doctor made a motion with his head, a private message meant for Rebecca, who gave a small nod and quickly crossed the room with the empty cup. "Tell me what year you think this is, son," the older man said gently.

"I know exactly what year this is…it's—" He cut himself short, not sure why, except if he gave the wrong answer they might think he *was* crazy and who knew what they'd do with him.

"Maybe I need to lie down again."

"I think it wise." Doc Davis helped him to his feet and then onto the cot. "We'll get some food in you later. But for now, it's important you keep drinking water."

Rebecca handed the doctor the tin cup, which he brought to Jake's lips. He knew the man was right. Judging by the desert that used to be his mouth, he was still dehydrated, which could easily cause mental confusion. He took a sip, but the water tasted nasty. Was that his imagination also? The cup was again tilted to his lips, and he swallowed.

"That should help you rest," the doctor said, as he guided Jake to a horizontal position. "We'll talk more later."

"Help me rest?" Shit. Not more morphine. Jake wanted to spit it out but it was too late. He knew the fog would descend soon. Maybe it already had started because he felt light-headed, or maybe it was his insane imagination playing with his mind.

He watched the doctor head for the door. Not the one that led outside, but a door Jake didn't recall noticing before. A narrow door just past the wood-burning stove.

"Rebecca?" He couldn't see her. Had she left, too?

"I'm here." She was beside him in a second, laying her cool hand on his arm.

"Stand where I can see you."

She moved to face him, her smile both sad and sweet.

He maneuvered his hand so that their palms met. "Tell me what year this is."

Her eyes widened slightly and the sadness overtook her face. "It's eighteen hundred and seventy-seven."

Doc Davis HAD LEFT at daybreak. There had been another hanging, Kitty had told Rebecca when she brought over a couple of biscuits for breakfast an hour ago. A rancher most of the townspeople knew was found dangling by his neck from a tree, but unlike the others who'd been hanged in the middle of the night over the past two months, Otis Sanford was still alive.

Using a rag, Rebecca removed the hot iron kettle from the fire and poured herself a cup of coffee. Her hand was shaky and she spilled some of the brew onto the floor. For the third night in a row, she hadn't slept well, but weariness wasn't what had her jittery. Worrying about Jake had her nerves frayed. He hadn't woken up since last evening. Had she given him too much medicine? She'd done just like the doctor had ordered, given him the exact amount she had before.

Or maybe Jake was sicker than Doc Davis thought. That's why he wasn't waking up. That's why he was so confused about where he was. Heaven help him, the poor man didn't even know what year this was. She sank onto the chair beside him, right where she'd kept vigil most of the night, in between dozing and reading. Wrapping her hands around the cup for warmth, she took a small sip.

Her gaze caught on the tin cup she kept on the table. She could've sworn she'd filled it. This was the second time the water seemed to have disappeared into thin air. Might be she was the one going mad. With her free hand, she pulled her shawl tighter around her shoulders. It didn't seem to matter how dutifully she'd tended the fire, the room hadn't warmed up. She hoped Jake was comfortable enough with the wool blanket she'd thrown over him.

She looked toward the foot of the cot where she'd carefully tucked in the edges to keep his feet warm. The blanket had come loose. Her heart beat faster. Had he moved without her seeing? Oh, how she wanted him to move, to open his eyes again, how she wanted to hear his low manly voice.

Rebecca liked Doc Davis. He was a smart, kind man

who was helping keep her out of the saloon, but she didn't care what he said, she wouldn't give Jake the medicine any more. It wasn't doing him any good. For four years she'd been taught something about medicine, too. Not the kind Doc Davis approved of, but she'd learned enough to know that Jake was better when he didn't drink it.

After setting down her coffee, she got up to fix the blanket. She'd tucked it under Jake's feet when she thought she saw his leg move. Her gaze flew to his face. His eyes were still closed.

"Jake?"

He didn't move.

Sniffing, she returned to sit in the chair and then pressed one of his large hands between hers. "Jake, please wake up. You have to eat something and drink more water."

She brought his hand up, laid her cheek against his palm and sighed at the feel of his slightly callused skin. Closing her eyes, she silently recited one of the childhood prayers she remembered.

He flexed his hand.

Rebecca stiffened, and then sharply drew back. She realized she was still holding his hand and dropped it. Her gaze went to his face. His eyes were open, but only to slits.

"Jake?"

"Is anyone else here?" he whispered.

She shook her head.

"Are you expecting the doctor or Kitty?"

"Not for a while."

"Good." He pushed his shoulders up off the cot.

She leaned forward to help, but realized he'd lifted himself with little effort. He sat up, pushed back the blanket and then swung his feet to the floor. He grimaced some, and groaned once, but he looked surprisingly strong.

"Where's my shirt?" he asked, lightly touching the last blister that was healing near the corner of his mouth.

"It's ruined. I tried to scrub it but the blood wouldn't come out." She watched with alarm as he reached for his boots, grabbing one but missing the other. "You aren't leaving."

"Damn right I am."

Panic gripped her. "Please, you should have some water. You should—"

Anger changed the blue of his eyes to a stormy gray. "You're not giving me any more of that crap."

"No," she agreed quietly, knowing he meant the pain medicine. "No more."

He eyed her with suspicion. "Didn't the doctor tell you to give me more?"

"Yes." She swallowed, and clasped her hands tightly together. "But I disobeyed him."

He studied her with an intensity that frightened her. "Why?"

"Because it made you wrong in the head."

Jake seemed to relax, then his chest rose and fell with a deep shuddering breath. "That's a very powerful drug, do you understand?"

She blinked, aware suddenly that she'd been gawking at his fine bare chest. Heat crawled up her neck, and she stared down at her hands.

"Rebecca? Do you understand that it's not bad medicine if someone really needs it? But I don't."

"I understand," she said. "I didn't like the way you acted, but I also know you still have pain."

"I do, but I'm healing, and I'll be better soon. Some of my symptoms were from the morphine, not the accident." He felt the side of his head, and then touched his finger to his lower lip. "My mouth is better. Did you put something on it?"

"Yes, I—" She couldn't admit to him that she'd used the sap from a cactus. It was good medicine, she knew from experience, but Doc Davis would be angry if he found out. "It was a salve," she said, only half lying. "I don't know the name. You said you had an accident. You remember what happened?"

"I think so." He paused, his gaze fixed on her face. "I was driving back to Houston, and my truck rolled."

"Oh." Disappointment washed over her. She'd truly hoped he was better, but even Doc Davis didn't know about this "truck."

"You honestly don't know what a truck is."

She shook her head.

Jake's expression turned grim. "I have one more question." He looked angry, confused and maybe even a bit afraid as he glanced about the room. Before he could ask his question, the pounding of horse hooves stopped just outside the door. Someone shouted Doc Davis's name. And then there was a gunshot.

5

JAKE FOLLOWED REBECCA to the window, but before she had the curtains parted, the door flew open. It was Kitty, looking startled when she saw Jake standing there, and then relieved as she flung the door wide.

"Glad to see you on your feet, Mr. Malone. It appears we're gonna need your cot." She picked up her skirts and swung back around to face outside. "Be real careful with him, boys."

Rebecca scurried to the side, holding onto the door, and Jake quickly pulled back the curtain to see who Kitty was talking to.

Three men hovered around an old wooden wagon hitched to a pair of bay mares. All of them wore dusty jeans, boots, hats and coats. Doc Davis was with them, his weathered face a mask of bleak concern, his black bag sitting on the street while he gestured with his hands.

Shaking his head, trying to clear his vision, Jake squeezed his eyes shut, almost afraid to open them again. When he did, the bizarre scene hadn't changed. The saloon across the street was still there, so was the rickety two-story hotel beside it, the water troughs and hitching rails in front, the wagon and horses, and the gun-toting cowboys of varying ages who were now carefully lifting someone out of the back of the wagon. The place looked like a stage.

"Make sure the way is clear," the doctor hollered at Kitty, who'd already entered the room. "And get the water boiling."

Rebecca didn't wait for further instructions. She grabbed the kettle off the fire and threw in a couple of logs. Kitty moved the chair that had been sitting beside the cot, dragging it to the far side of the room. Next she got rid of the basin and bedside table. No one said a word. Like a well-oiled machine, the two women worked quickly, preparing the cot, putting water on to heat and producing stacks of clean rags.

Jake simply stayed out of their way. When the cowboys finally carried in the injured man, Jake moved further back to allow them a clear shot to the cot.

Davis followed close behind, his face grimy and his coat muddy. He slanted a look at Jake. "Glad to see you up and about, son," he said, and hurried past to tend to the new patient.

After the man was laid down, and the doctor was at his side, Kitty took charge of dispersing the cowboys. They all seemed reluctant to leave, but none of them challenged her when she ordered them to wait outside or in the saloon. After being assured that they'd be given a full report, they grudgingly filed out the door.

Rebecca had retreated to the corner and stayed there while the men were in the room. On his way out, one of the younger cowboys tipped his hat to her, to which she gave a small nod, but other than that, she mostly kept her gaze aimed at the floor. Her hands stayed clasped in front of her. The guy called Corbin had implied she was a whore. As soon as Jake was back to normal, he had a score to settle with the stupid bastard.

Thinking about Corbin reminded Jake of the badge he thought he'd seen pinned to the guy's vest. That was another question he had for Rebecca as soon as he had her to himself again.

"This doesn't look good." The doctor yanked open the unconscious man's shirt and took a wet cloth Kitty handed him.

"Is he breathing?" Kitty asked.

"Barely. Open my bag and get out my stethoscope, would you?"

Jake had never been the queasy type, but when he saw what the rope had done to the man's thick neck his stomach revolted. Raw flesh gaped almost to the bone, the skin looking more like something that came from a butchered heifer.

Jake must have looked as if he was going to lose it, because Rebecca was instantly by his side, slipping an arm around his waist, helping to support his weight.

"You're very pale," she whispered.

"I haven't eaten in days," he said gruffly, his ego bruised, and now, on top of everything, he was light-headed.

She held him tighter when he sagged against her. "I'll heat some broth as soon as I won't be in the way."

"I'm okay." He shifted closer to the wall in case he needed it to keep himself steady. "Go help the doctor. That guy on the cot is in a lot worse shape than I am."

"Kitty's there." She stared up at him, with her beautiful blue-green eyes full of concern. Not a speck of makeup marred her flawless skin. She looked so damn young and innocent. "Do you need to sit down?"

"Am I crushing you?"

A small smile tugged at her pink lips. "I'm very strong."

"I've noticed."

Her nose wrinkled and any trace of a smile vanished. "Like an ox, I've been told."

Jake chuckled. "Not even close."

She tilted her head to the side slightly, and gazed at him with a cute bewildered expression.

"Rebecca, I need some of that heated water." Kitty threw a look over her shoulder, and frowned at Jake. "Need to sit?"

"I'm fine."

Rebecca seemed reluctant to leave him, so he gave her a gentle nudge.

"Go," he told her, touched that she was so protective of him. He was the one who looked out for people, not the other way around. "I promise not to keel over."

She pursed her lips in a disapproving pout, then hurried to the stove.

"We'll get some food into your belly shortly," Kitty said, from a kneeling position on the floor, while dividing her attention between him and the other man. "That'll help steady you. In the meantime, plant yourself in that chair."

Jake knew she was right. At this point, most of his weakness probably had more to do with lack of food, and if he wanted to get out of here he needed to regain his strength. Aware that Rebecca kept a watchful eye on his progress, he slowly moved toward the chair, trying not to wince when his head started to throb.

She carried the bowl of water to Kitty. "It's only warm."

"Good enough." Kitty dropped a white cloth into the bowl, and then set it on the floor beside her. "I need to bathe the wounds without them getting infected."

Doc Davis's heartfelt sigh echoed off the walls of the

small room. "After that, there's nothing more to do but wait and pray he wakes up."

"Pray." Kitty scoffed. "You still believe there's a God after what we've seen lately. Even if poor Otis does wake up, you think he's gonna be right in the head?"

"No telling at this point," the doctor said dismally. "Those vigilantes have gone too far this time. Otis Sanford never harmed a hair on anyone's head. He's no more a rustler than I am."

"Neither were Tom Lancaster or Homer Cook, if you ask me," Kitty added. "And you know I wasn't none too fond of Homer, so that's saying something."

"Rustling?" That had gotten Jake's attention.

"Been a problem for the past two months." The doctor removed his wire-rimmed glasses and rubbed his eyes. "Six ranches have lost most of their herds."

"And those lousy good-for-nothing Rangers haven't done a damn thing to stop it," Kitty said as she gathered her skirt in one hand and struggled to her feet.

The doctor lent her a hand, his voice lowering as he cautioned, "Watch your mouth, Kitty. Even you don't want Wade to hear you saying that. He hasn't been in very good spirits, and you know as well as anyone he can be mean even when he is."

Kitty's red-painted lips pulled into a thin line, a trace of resentment flickering in her eyes. But she said nothing more.

"These Rangers," Jake said. "Do they come to town often?"

All three of them stared at him in surprise, but it was Kitty who, with undisguised contempt, said, "Honey, those boys run this town."

The doctor looked resigned. Rebecca's expression mirrored Kitty's.

"Texas Rangers don't 'run' towns," Jake said, tamping down the defensiveness tightening his chest. Now wasn't the time to get into a debate no matter how clearheaded he felt. Better to just listen and sort out what was happening later. "Don't you have a sheriff?"

Kitty snorted, while the doctor's mouth curved in a patronizing smile. Rebecca's gaze was on the other two as if she were waiting for an answer, as well.

"We did once," Kitty said, "but what happened to him is still a mystery. The next day after he disappeared, the Rangers showed up. That was near three years ago. Not too hard to figure that one out."

The doctor stared at her, his face creased in a perplexed frown. "I don't understand you talking about Wade like that."

"Wade came later. I'm talking about Corbin."

"Nevertheless, enough of that kind of talk, you hear? We don't need trouble." He stooped down to pick up his bag. "If you two ladies will be kind enough to take turns keeping an eye on Otis, I believe I'll get some rest."

"Land's sakes, it's a wonder you're still standing." Kitty made a shooing motion. "You've been up for over twenty-four hours. Now go."

"Bossy woman," the doctor muttered. "It's a wonder you ever have any customers."

"I could always use one more." Kitty winked at him, and laughed when he gave her a long-suffering shake of his head.

Selfishly, Jake wanted the doctor to stick around and answer a few questions because he'd likely be more helpful than either of the two women. Hell, he had a lot more than a few questions, but until he figured out what was going on, he needed to stay low key.

Doc Davis stopped and gave Jake a once-over. "You're

looking better, son. Still, sorry to have to kick you out of your bed. I have only two other rooms, one is my office where I see patients, and the other is my living quarters. Kitty, you know if there's room at the boardinghouse?"

"Honey, don't you worry about handsome here. There's room over the saloon. Me and the girls will take care of him."

"*I'll* take care of Jake," Rebecca said in a prickly tone that drew all eyes to her. She blushed. "I only meant that there's no need to bother the other girls."

"True enough," the doctor said with an amused glint in his eyes. He sobered just as quickly. "I forgot that I'm turning you out, too."

"Don't you fret none, Doc. I have a place where neither of them will be bothered." Kitty gave him a gentle shove. "You get some rest."

"I suppose we could put Otis in my room," the doctor murmured absently.

"Hush, you old fool. You're not gonna do nobody any good if you start ailing because you're bone tired," Kitty said with gruff affection, and escorted him through the narrow door past the stove.

As soon as they were gone, Rebecca went straight to the stove, removed a kettle and set a pot over the fire. Then she busily began picking up rags, tidying up the ointment and bandages the doctor had left, and then mopping up where water had sloshed over the rim of the basin.

Jake watched her work, his thoughts splintering in several directions. He felt good, mentally at least. No more brain fog or blurred vision. He was still dehydrated but not as badly as yesterday. A few times when Rebecca had dozed off in the middle of the night, he'd slipped out of bed and helped himself to the water she kept in the white pitcher. And then he'd bided his time, waiting for the morphine to completely leave his system before he let her know he was awake. He didn't blame her for giving him the drug. She'd only been following the doctor's orders.

Even his memory had improved considerably, to the point that he recalled being ordered out of his truck by one of Wellesly's thugs, shot at, and then rolling his truck into the desert. The only murky part in his recollection was the couple of minutes before he'd blacked out, the sense of drowning he'd experienced, as though he were being sucked down by a powerful ocean undercurrent. Right. In the middle of the desert.

But even that weirdness didn't account for his inability to reconcile what he'd witnessed in the past twenty-four hours. Or these people's claim that they were living in 1877. Was this some sort of cult where they'd been brainwashed? He was actually beginning to believe that *they* believed they lived in the past. Hell, someone had actually tried to hang that poor bastard.

The one thing he had trouble with was the location. Texas was a big state, but not so big that these people could be isolated from the truth. Hell, they'd have to have seen a plane fly overhead at some point, or wander far enough away from town to run across a normal human being or a highway or an ATV or a dirt bike. Nowadays the rich kids were always looking for new places to ride their toys.

There was another possibility. He'd hit his head hard enough that he'd gone friggin' crazy. This whole thing could be one big hallucination. While the accident was now vivid, the past twenty-four hours not so much.

"I hope it's hot enough." Rebecca broke into his thoughts, holding out a steaming bowl cradled in a white cloth. "It's chicken broth."

She had beautiful eyes, the greenish-blue a color he'd only seen in the Caribbean ocean where he'd learned to dive three years ago. And her lips, perfectly bow-shaped, plump and pink… Man, he so didn't want Rebecca to be a hallucination.

Her brows drew together in a delicate frown. "If you hold this, I'll bring the stool to set the bowl on."

"What? Oh, sorry." He took the bowl from her, the aroma from the broth drifting up to his nose, and making his stomach growl loudly.

Rebecca turned away, but not before he saw her smile. "Kitty brought me biscuits for breakfast. If you think your belly will take it, you can dunk them in the broth." She set the stool in front of him, and then brought him a small cloth-wrapped bundle.

Her gaze lowered to his chest, and she quickly looked away. He'd forgotten he wasn't wearing a shirt, though there wasn't much he could do about it.

"I assume there's a store in town." He picked up the spoon, suddenly famished. "Where I can buy a new shirt?"

She blinked. "I don't expect the general store sells ready-made shirts."

He spooned some broth into his mouth, surprised at how tasty it was, and did everything he could not to pick up the bowl and slurp down the whole thing in one gulp. She unwrapped the cloth napkin for him and offered the two biscuits. He eagerly took one, not caring that it was as hard as a rock, and dunked it into the broth. It softened some, but he was too impatient to wait and bit into the firm little puck.

"Don't eat too fast," Rebecca cautioned with a gentle hand on his arm. "You need to keep the food down."

He nodded, his gaze lingering on her tiny wrist and hand. As fragile as she seemed, her hands were working hands, with small nicks and faded scars on the backs of her knuckles. Made him wonder about the scar he'd seen on her wrist, concealed now by her cuff.

She quickly withdrew, hiding her hands in the folds of her skirt. "Kitty should be back soon," she said unnecessarily, and then moistened her lips. "She'll take you to the saloon."

"Why?" He set down the spoon.

"There's no room here."

"No, I mean, why Kitty? Why not you?"

Rebecca's gaze went to the window, fear haunting her face. "I have to stay with Mr. Otis."

"Do you know him?"

She glanced over her shoulder at the unconscious man lying in the corner, and shook her head.

"Kitty knows him. Let her stay." He was being totally selfish, he knew, but he didn't want to leave Rebecca. He didn't want her to leave him.

She wrung her hands together, her gaze nervously darting around the room. "You'll have to wear your stained shirt for now but it's clean. I can make you another one. If Kitty will get me some fabric, I'll start this afternoon."

"Rebecca." He set the bowl down on the stool, half the biscuit still floating in the broth. "What's wrong?" He started to reach for her but she looked so distraught, he stopped himself. The last thing he wanted to do was spook her. "Did I say something wrong?"

She visibly swallowed. "No. I don't like going to the saloon." She stared down at the bowl. "You have to eat. Get strong. Leave this town as fast as you can."

The quiet desperation in her voice really got to him. "Why?"

She bit her lip. "Kitty says I talk too much."

He smiled. "Right."

Distrust lurked in the depths of her eyes, but damned if

he knew how he earned that. "You smiled," she said softly, and he realized it wasn't distrust but surprise.

"I did."

"I like your smile. It's nice." She was an interesting contradiction. Strong as steel one minute, and childlike the next.

"How old are you?"

"Twenty-four."

Pretty young, although he'd guessed younger. Maybe because she was so tiny. "You have family here?"

"No." Abruptly she turned away and began folding rags from a heap on the dresser. "You must eat."

He got the hint. No more personal questions. Fine. He had more important ones. He picked up the spoon, scooped up some of the soggy biscuit and shoveled it into his mouth. "I smelled coffee earlier. Any left?"

"I put the kettle back on the fire. The coffee should be hot soon."

"What do you people have against microwaves?"

Rebecca stopped folding and frowned at him.

"Right. You don't know what a car or truck or microwave is." His annoyance ebbed when he saw the hurt in her eyes. Apparently she had no trouble understanding sarcasm. "What is that?" he asked, nudging his chin at what looked like a pamphlet that had been hidden under the pile of rags.

She followed his gaze, and when she saw what he was looking at, sighed. "It's Kitty's. She wants me to learn about society." Rebecca slightly stumbled over the word, as though it were foreign to her.

That alone drew Jake's interest. He'd only wanted to change the subject, but he stared at the thin publication that looked like a magazine supplement. His pulse picked up speed. If Kitty was concerned about Rebecca learning about society, that supported his theory that this was a cloistered religious sect or cult. Maybe that's why Rebecca had urged him to leave here as fast as he could. Maybe she wanted to go with him.

"May I see it?" he asked casually.

Rebecca giggled. "It's for ladies."

Jake smiled. "I know."

She hesitated, and then passed it to him, her cheeks turning pink. "I'll get the coffee."

The publication consisted of one large sheet folded in half to make four pages. The printing was crude, and the title read *Home Journal.* Published in 1877.

Jake blinked, thinking, hoping he wasn't seeing clearly, but his vision was just fine. Okay, so the periodical looked new and in good shape, but that didn't mean it didn't belong to a collector.

He scanned the small room, his heart pounding faster as he absorbed small details like the shelf of castor oil and two bottles labeled calomel and jalap, a package of mustard plaster, and for the first time he really got it. This wasn't a modern-day religious sect, or even an elaborate hoax.

Someway, somehow, he'd fallen through a wormhole, or a portal or a nightmare, and had spiraled through time, ending up in 1877 Texas, one of the worst periods in Ranger history.

The thought chilled him.

6

JAKE SQUINTED as the brisk air blew down Main Street and
stung his face. The town wasn't much. A two-story hotel
butted up to the saloon which took up the entire corner of
the dirt street. Three other rickety wooden buildings Jake
couldn't identify separated the general store and telegraph
office from a rambling white clapboard structure that Kitty
pointed out as Isabella's boardinghouse.

Even if Jake wanted to deny the mounting evidence that
he had somehow crossed a time barrier, the pungent earthy
smells hovering over the dreary town would undercut his
rebuttal. Good thing he had a strong stomach.

They stepped from the sagging, creaky boardwalk into
the street, Rebecca supporting Jake on the right, while
Kitty stayed close on his left. The light meal he'd eaten
had revived him considerably, and he didn't need the help,
but for Rebecca's sake, he said nothing. Clearly, she hadn't
wanted to leave Doc Davis's place, and although she tried
to hide her fear, Jake felt the tension radiating from her
body.

A man approached on horseback, not bothering to slow
down as he passed, and left them in a wake of dust. Kitty
sputtered and swore. Man, she had a mouth on her.

In front of the saloon, Kitty stopped to dust herself off and fix her upswept hair. Rebecca clung tighter to his arm, and stared warily at a pair of geldings tied to a hitching rail.

Kitty apparently sensed her apprehension, and said, "That roan belongs to Will Stevens, a boy that works for Otis. He's probably hanging around to find out how his boss is doing." She shook her head. "But I don't reckon Doc is going to know anything until tomorrow. As far as the other horse, I don't know who it belongs to, but it's okay, honey. It's early. The saloon's quiet."

Rebecca didn't reply, just straightened her spine and lifted her chin.

Damn, Jake hated depending on them, or anyone. He'd checked his pocket, and his wallet and cash were still there, but his currency meant nothing. Not in 1877. He still couldn't believe this was happening. What was worse, being crazy, or getting sucked back into time? The jury was still out on that one.

"Wait," he said just as Kitty was about to push open the swinging saloon doors. "This woman who runs the boardinghouse, you think she might let me stay there in exchange for doing some work around the place?"

Kitty's brows raised in surprise. "Sugar, you're not well enough to be doing much of anything. Anyway, Isabella's all full up. Come the end of the week, the hotel will be, too. Word is that we got some railroad men coming." She looked apologetically at Rebecca. "We'll all be mighty busy then."

Rebecca made a small sound of distress that Kitty either didn't hear or chose to ignore, as she guided them through the doors of the saloon.

Jake found Rebecca's hand and gave it a light squeeze. He felt like crap for putting her through this. He wasn't sure what was going on with her, and he'd been too wrapped up in his own problem to pay much attention. But he had a feeling her fear had a lot to do with the Rangers.

Which really killed him. Modern Rangers were held in high esteem. They were an elite few, the cream that rose to the top. Not only were hundreds of applicants turned down each year, most of them were well-qualified applicants. To be a Texas Ranger really meant something. But he was also aware of the agency's tarnished history. Corruption and brutality had blemished their name for a brief stint in time. Just his luck that's where he ended up.

They stepped into the dimly lit saloon, crowded with wooden tables and empty chairs, and on one wall, an oil painting of a half-naked woman. At the back was a staircase leading to a balcony and a series of doors. Only three people were in the place, the bald bartender and two customers sitting at the bar, all of whom turned their way as soon as they came through the swinging door. The disinterested bartender went back to polishing a glass. One of the two cowboys stared anxiously at Kitty while slowly pulling off his hat.

She shook her head at him. "Sorry, Will, nothing yet," she told the tall lanky kid not quite out of his teens. "I reckon Doc Davis will know something tomorrow."

As if to hide his grief-stricken face, he abruptly went back to his beer.

The second cowboy really pissed Jake off. The older man turned away from the bar and leaned back against it, elbows up while insolently checking out Rebecca. His mouth curved in a lewd smile and he made a kissing sound as they passed him.

She tensed, and Jake jerked away from the women, intent on facing the bastard. Kitty quickly grabbed his arm, the back of her wrist jabbing against his ribs. Pain shot through him. He struggled to catch his breath, doing everything in his power to keep from doubling over.

"What's wrong with you?" she snarled, and hurried them past the piano toward the stairs. "You start chasing away customers, and Captain Wade will put a bullet right between those pretty blue eyes of yours."

Jake muttered a curse. From the pain. But mostly from feeling so damn helpless. He knew his ribs weren't broken, but they were badly bruised. He didn't care, because he knew he'd heal, but he was useless to Rebecca. Unless he could get his hands on a gun.

She looped an arm through his. "Once we get upstairs, you can stay there," she said, her voice soft and pleading. "No one will bother you."

"I'm not worried about me."

Rebecca's eyes remained carefully noncommittal as they met his. "You need to rest."

"Come on, you two. Get your asses upstairs." The usually unflappable Kitty seemed agitated. "I'll be up after I grab a bottle of whiskey. Rebecca, you know which room."

She picked up her skirt so that the hem cleared the stairs, and promptly took the lead with remarkable agility. Jake still smarted from the jab to his ribs and had to use the handrail, but he wasn't in so much pain that he didn't notice her slim ankles and the sexy curve of her calf.

"So, that's him." The unfamiliar feminine voice came from the balcony.

Jake looked up to see three women in various stages of undress, leaning over the railing, sizing him up. The one with the dark hair, olive skin and abundant cleavage flashed him a flirtatious grin. "You can stay in my room, *amante,*" she said with a slight Spanish accent. "Lola will take very good care of you."

The other two blond women laughed. They all seemed to be in their midtwenties, but it was hard to tell for sure with the heavy black makeup around their eyes and their garishly red tinted lips.

"Ruby, did ya get those sheets changed?" Kitty had already made it to the end of the bar, where the bartender had set down a bottle of booze and a couple of glasses.

The taller, thinner blonde, wearing what Jake assumed were bloomers and a corset, twirled a long tendril of hair around her finger. "Yes, ma'am, I did." She winked at Jake, and then switched her attention to the men at the bar. "You boys gonna drink all day, or you wanna come up and visit me and Trixie."

Jake didn't see the men's reaction, but they apparently weren't interested because Ruby shrugged and leaned one hip against the rail while she watched Rebecca lead Jake to the second door.

"When you get better, you come see me," the blonde said. "I'm the fifth door." She gave him a bored smile, sashayed to the end of the balcony and then disappeared behind the designated door.

Five doors, five women. His insides coiling like a spring, he looked at Rebecca. She kept her face averted, but he saw her hand tremble as she turned the doorknob. So it hadn't been the morphine confusing him, and Corbin hadn't been blowing smoke when he'd called Rebecca a whore. Damn.

REBECCA HADN'T BEEN in her room for over a week. Not that she even considered it her room. She'd only used it for three nights after the Rangers had first brought her to Diablo Flats. Nothing here belonged to her. Not the hard narrow bed, or small dresser missing a drawer, or the washbasin and towels. She didn't even own the hairbrush or borrowed red dress draped over the poorly made oak stool.

Even the dress on her back belonged to Trixie, who was two inches taller and ten pounds heavier. Out of the corner of her eye, she noticed a pair of unmentionables hanging on the back of the door. Mortified, she quickly snatched the ruffled white pantalets off the hook and balled them up behind her back before Jake could see them.

"Who does this room belong to?" he asked, his gaze going to the chamber pot shoved halfway under the bed, before returning to her face. He looked disappointed, almost as if he'd already passed judgment over an answer she'd not yet given.

She took a deep breath. "No one." She wasn't lying. Not really.

"Who does that dress belong to?"

"Trixie."

He seemed surprised. "But this isn't her room."

Rebecca shook her head. "I'll fetch some water," she said, scooping the dress off the stool. "Cook is making beans and cornbread for supper, but if you're still hungry I'll check if there's more biscuits and broth."

"Rebecca."

She tried to move past him to the door but he blocked her way. She stared at the floor. "I won't be long."

"I'm not judging you."

That made her look up. "I don't understand."

"I know what you do. How you make your living. I imagine it's difficult being a woman alone here."

Their eyes met, briefly, and then she had to look away. He could deny his disappointment but she saw it lurking in his eyes. He didn't understand her situation, how she'd ended up in this hellhole, but to explain to him would make everything worse. If he knew where she'd been, what she'd done, he'd hate her. He'd push her as far away as he could.

He hooked his finger under her chin and lifted her face to his. "Thank you for taking care of me."

She couldn't speak. How could he be so kind? How could there be tenderness in his eyes when he knew what she was?

Kitty had warned her. Men treated whores differently than other women, some men even treated their horses better than they did a whore. But not Jake...he was kind and gentle and...

Oh, God. The sting of tears pricked the back of Rebecca's eyes. She quickly lowered her lids, but it was too late. Jake used his thumb to wipe away the moisture that seeped from the corner.

"Ah, Rebecca, am I making you cry?"

She shook her head. "I'm not crying," she whispered, her voice thin and uncertain.

"Okay." He smiled. And then he lowered his head and touched his lips to hers. Lightly, as light as the wings of a butterfly.

To her amazement, she leaned toward him, her entire body responding to the gentle kiss. She hadn't even known she'd moved until she found her palms flat against his chest and the heels of her boots off the floor. He slanted his head ever so slightly, his lips parting. Rebecca strained a bit higher, her sudden eagerness sending a tingle down to her toes. She felt her own lips parting, her eyes drifting closed.

Her boldness shocked her. Shamed her to her core. She stumbled backward, and in her haste, shoved him away harder than she'd intended. Without looking at his face, she hastened out the door. Jake was a decent man, like none she'd ever met. She'd been made a whore, and he hadn't judged her for it. But how forgiving would he be if he learned she'd been an Indian's whore?

KITTY SET the tray of whiskey and beer on the table to pass out to the three men. Impatient as always, Corbin picked up a shot off the tray, brought it to his lips and threw his head back. Some of the liquor, along with half his supper, ended up in his shaggy beard. He was a revolting pig, and she could barely stand to set eyes on him anymore.

Bart and Moses exchanged looks of disgust, but neither man said anything. They left Corbin alone when Wade wasn't around to keep tempers from burning too hot. He didn't even have to try. Nobody crossed Wade, plain and simple. Even when Corbin was drunk, he had enough sense to keep his mouth shut when the boss was around.

The other two men each nodded at Kitty as she set their beer and whiskeys in front of them. She purposely gave Corbin his beer last, and he slid her an evil look letting her know she'd pissed him off.

She didn't give a shit. Sure, she had a couple more lines around her eyes and her bosom wasn't as firm as it once was, but Wade still visited her more than he did the other girls. They had a history, her and Wade, that went clear back to San Antonio. He told her things he wouldn't tell another living soul. Mostly because he understood she knew how to keep her mouth shut. Could be he even knew that in spite of everything that was going on around Diablo Flats, she still loved him.

"It ain't right him staying upstairs with the whore." Corbin picked up his mug of beer and chugged half of it down. "Bad for business. How can she make us any money?"

Kitty picked up the tray. "Jake isn't well enough to travel or fend for himself."

"You think I give a shit about that?" Corbin glared at her with such hatred she got a bit weak in the knees. "Get me more whiskey. And bring the goddamn bottle this time."

His voice boomed off the walls. A couple of heads turned, and then the men went back to staring at their beer. Like every Saturday night, the saloon was crowded with cowpunchers who worked at the nearby ranches. Normally the boys tended to get rowdy, but tonight everyone wore long faces and talked quietly amongst themselves. So far, only Lola had snared a customer, one of the drifters who was headed south to the border and had remarked on the place looking like a funeral parlor.

Kitty figured the downcast mood was on account of what happened to Otis last night. Folks admired him because he was an honorable man, generous with the boys that worked for him and with neighbors who needed a helping hand. Then, too, everyone likely was worried about who might get strung up next.

Trixie and Ruby were watching the card players, and when Kitty glanced over at them, Ruby took her meaning and went to the bar to get a bottle.

"There's no room at Doc's for Jake," Kitty said casually. "Otis is laid up there."

Bart and Moses gave each other quick looks under the rims of their hats, and finished their shots.

Glaring at her, Corbin spit in a spittoon three feet away, not caring that he'd missed.

"Too bad about what happened to him." Kitty ignored the vulgar man and planted a hand on her hip, easy like, showing him he didn't rile her none. Letting him smell weakness would be bad. "Makes a body wonder who these vigilantes are. Everyone from around here knows Otis is no rustler."

"I told you to get me my damn whiskey." Corbin leaned close, spit flying from his mouth. "I ain't gonna tell—"

Ruby set the bottle in front of him.

He grabbed her wrist and twisted it until she whimpered. "I didn't ask you, now did I?"

Kitty picked up the bottle, ready to smash it across his head. "Let her go."

Corbin stared at her with a look of disbelief, that inched into a feral smile.

"Come on now, Kitty, ain't no need for this." Bart touched her arm. "Corbin, let go of Ruby."

Corbin locked gazes with Kitty for another few seconds, and then flung Ruby toward the next table. She caught the back of a chair, saving herself from ending up on the hard plank floor. Sending the back of Corbin's head a resentful look, she fixed her bodice and then scurried to the bar.

Kitty reluctantly set the bottle back on the table. "You know Wade don't take to you hurting the girls."

"Shut up, Kitty," Bart said in a hushed voice, his normally ruddy face dark with warning.

She heeded his counsel. Bart wasn't one to interfere unless there was big trouble on the horizon. Could be Corbin had been drinking more than Kitty realized.

Behind her, she heard the door to the saloon open and then Wade's voice, and allowed herself a small victorious smile. Corbin wouldn't bother her with Wade here.

"Ain't you the lucky lazy-ass whore," Corbin mumbled as he uncapped the bottle.

She adjusted her skirt and touched her hair, before turning around. Wade had stopped at the bar, but now he strode toward her, his duster flapping against his long legs as he walked. His black hair, graying at the temples, was damp from his bath, and swept away from his lean clean-shaven face. Funny how he could still make her heart flutter after all these years.

"Don't you look pretty tonight, Kitty." He winked and kissed her cheek, before pulling out a chair.

She smiled, mostly because he said the same thing every night he was in town. Which was happening less and less lately. Sometimes he was gone for days. Patrolling the border and hunting rustlers, or so he claimed. Kitty had her doubts. Not that she would ever voice them.

He removed his hat and sat down. "You boys eat yet?"

Bart and Moses nodded. Corbin didn't answer.

She touched Wade's shoulder. "I'll get you a glass, honey."

He caught her hand as it started to trail away. "Lloyd's telling Cook to fry me up a steak, and then he's bringing me a beer." He glanced at Bart and Moses, but then set his sights on Corbin. "You boys take it easy on the whiskey. We ride before sunup."

Bart shifted uncomfortably.

Moses snorted with disgust. "But Boss, me and the boys are tired. We've been out for five nights straight and—"

Wade slammed his hand on the table, making the glasses rattle. He pierced Moses with a steely-eyed warning. "I don't recall asking for your opinion," he said in a calm voice. He had a powerful enough temper, although it didn't show much. At six-four and as fast as he was with a gun, he generally didn't have to ask for anything twice.

Moses looked pissed, but he knew enough to keep his mouth shut. He finished his drink and then scraped back from the table. "Then I best get some sleep."

"Sit down, honey," Wade said to Kitty, and kicked out the chair Moses had left empty. "Have a glass of whiskey with us."

Kitty sat and reached for the bottle. Though she'd much

rather have Wade to herself, she normally didn't mind sitting with him and the boys for a spell. But not tonight. The murderous way Corbin was staring at her put her on edge. Naturally he'd never let Wade catch him, but she knew there was something no good going on in that small wicked brain of his.

"Glad you're here, Kitty," Corbin said. "Time to let Wade know what's going on up there with that squaw whore."

Wade leaned forward, his hand shooting out to grab Corbin's wrist. Whiskey sloshed out of his glass onto the table. Keeping his voice low, Wade said, "Keep your fucking mouth shut. No one talks about where we got her. Who's gonna pay for pussy that's been had by an Indian?"

Corbin yanked his arm away. "She ain't spread her legs for no one yet." He glared at Kitty. "You keep sending her over to Doc's instead of keeping her upstairs where she can make us some money."

Wade frowned, his gaze narrowing on Kitty. "That true?"

Kitty deliberately shrugged one shoulder, slowly, coyly, leaning toward Wade, and drawing his attention to the deep V of her purple dress. "Doc's been busy and needed someone. All the other girls have their regulars. You always tell me to keep Doc happy so he'll stick around to patch y'all up when you need it."

Corbin swore viciously. "But that ain't the worse part. Now she's got some pretty boy staying up there with her."

Wade's face darkened. "What?"

Kitty smiled prettily. "It's not what you think. Doc has Otis in his sickroom, and no bed for another patient. And this Jake fella is still sick, with his head and side hurt."

"So?"

"Isabella has no room at the boardinghouse, the hotel

is gonna be full up with the railroad people, and Doc still needs to look in on him from time to time."

"Shit." Wade looked at her as if she'd gone loco. "I don't care."

"Look, honey, I was thinking of you when I promised Doc we'd look after him here." She ignored Corbin's gloating stare and ran her hand suggestively up Wade's thigh. "Jake didn't have a gun or horse when Slow Jim found him. No money neither. He can't recall what happened. But he's big and strong and smart, and I figured with you being down a man since Lefty got himself killed, you might need another gun."

"This is bullshit, Boss." Corbin looked nervous. "If he's hurt, he ain't gonna do us no good."

"He's healing real fast," Kitty said quickly. "And he's good with a gun. I saw him grab Doc's Colt so fast when he got spooked that it damn near made my head spin." God help her, she hoped she wasn't lying about him being good with a gun.

"Hmm." Wade thoughtfully pursed his lips. "And he said he wanted work?"

She shrugged. "Claims he'd be willing to do anything."

Corbin snorted. "How do we know we can trust him?"

"We don't." Wade took a considering sip of beer. "We'll have to be real careful, is all. Until we know that we can."

Kitty breathed with relief, glad that Lloyd showed up with Wade's steak and potatoes at that moment. The bartender set the plate down and asked if anyone needed anything else. Kitty shook her head, kept her eyes on him and then Wade, anywhere but on Corbin. She'd won. He'd lost. He was going to be out for blood.

She hadn't meant to push him. It would do her no good to have Corbin watching her every move. At least not until Jake Malone was back on his feet and could get the hell out of here. He seemed a decent enough fella, and she hoped her gut feeling wasn't wrong about him. Though he wasn't her chief concern. It was Rebecca she cared about. The poor girl would die here if she didn't get out soon.

Oh, how much she reminded Kitty of herself when she'd been young and naïve and still full of hope. But it was much too late for her to crawl out of this snake pit. Not so for Rebecca. In some crazy way, if Kitty could help liberate her, she felt a small piece of herself would be free, as well.

7

THE CRICK in Jake's neck jarred him awake. He opened his eyes and gingerly turned his head, squinting when his face fell into the path of the sun streaming in through the part in the curtains. For a second he forgot where he was, that he was no longer convalescing in the doctor's sickroom, as Kitty and Rebecca called it.

Rebecca. This was her room.

He patted the empty bed beside him, caught a peripheral view of his shirt hanging on the door hook. Ignoring the pain in his neck, he forced his head to turn some more. Then he saw her, or at least he saw a mass of blond loopy curls spread over a blue-and-yellow patchwork quilt covering the floor.

"Rebecca?" He sat up, flexing his neck and shoulders.

She stirred, her small form curling into an even tighter ball.

Damn, had she slept on the hard floor all night? He couldn't remember the exact time they'd gone to sleep last night. They'd eaten a small dinner of beans and cornbread, and then she'd disappeared to wash some clothes while he lay on the bed, nursing his side, listening to the tinny strains of a badly played piano coming from the saloon below. She'd been gone awhile, long enough for him to start worrying that she'd ditched him.

Not that he would've blamed her. He hadn't had any business kissing her. No matter how brief and nonthreatening the kiss. He didn't want her to think that he felt her profession gave him permission to take what he wanted. She had to run into enough scummy men like that. How vulnerable she had to feel. The thought sickened him. For Rebecca, and for any woman with no family or husband in these times.

He'd been about to pull on his boots and go looking for her when she'd returned to the room with damp hair and smelling like roses. Made him crave a long hot shower. He'd settled for a rough cloth, horrible-smelling soap and a basin full of cool water.

He swung his feet to the floor, careful not to stomp on her. "Rebecca?"

She moved, stretched out an arm, and then slowly rolled over to blink blearily at him. Her eyes widened for a second, almost as if she'd forgotten he was there, and then she smiled shyly and yawned. She quickly covered her mouth and got up on her knees.

"I don't remember falling asleep," he said, feeling like crap. She didn't even have a pillow. "I didn't mean to hog the bed. Did you sleep down there all night?"

"I like sleeping on the floor."

"Right."

"I do." She gave him an indignant look, her gaze haltingly sliding to his bare chest. "Even at Doc Davis's I sleep on the floor. I haven't slept in a bed for—" She shoved the hair away from her face, and turned away, shuttering her eyes, while she straightened her dress, but too late to hide the faint rosiness seeping into her complexion.

"Look, tonight, if I'm still here, *I'm* sleeping on the floor."

She abruptly turned back to him with genuine concern. "Where else would you be?"

"I'm feeling pretty good, and I'll have to strike out on my own sooner or later. Can't stay here forever."

She bit her lip, gathered her hair in one hand, and then pulled it back into a loose braid. "Where will you go?" she asked, keeping her eyes averted.

"I'm not sure."

He'd thought about that for a good part of the evening as he'd watched her work by the light of a lantern, quietly letting out the cuffs of a shirt for him. He hadn't asked her where she'd found the brown shirt, and she hadn't volunteered. Bottom line was, he couldn't afford to be choosy. The bloodstains on his own blue chambray shirt weren't going to come out, and he didn't need calling unnecessary attention to himself. He did wish he knew what had happened to his watch and cell phone, though. His bomber jacket, too. Damn, it was his favorite one.

Rebecca had gotten to her feet and was folding the quilt, sending him curious sidelong glances.

He rose to help her fold the bulky comforter. "This guy Slow Jim who found me, is he back yet?"

"I don't know." Her fingers accidentally brushed his, and she quickly withdrew, yanking the quilt from him.

Great. He'd scared her with the damn kiss. Should he bring it up? Apologize? Promise he wouldn't do it again? Explain that it had meant nothing, that all he'd wanted was to... He sighed, scrubbed at his face, scratched his chest. No, he'd better not explain what he'd wanted. His overture hadn't started out sexual in nature, but as soon as their lips touched, as soon as he'd scented her warm sweet skin, his body had reacted, all right. Good to know that the important parts still worked just fine.

He finished rubbing his eyes and looked at her. She was staring at his chest. And not because she seemed offended by his partial nudity. Her look was one of pure feminine appreciation. That got his parts moving again.

Hell, not good.

He bent over and pretended to look for his boots. The sudden movement was a mistake. His head was still tender, and it didn't take much to restart the throbbing. Or maybe this was the after-effects of the whiskey from last night. He'd only drunk two shots because the stuff tasted like crap. Surprisingly potent, though. Maybe that's what had made him sleep so soundly. God, he couldn't believe he'd let her sleep on the floor.

"This is why you can't leave. Sit down," she said gruffly. "Is it bleeding again?"

He realized that he'd automatically put a hand to his temple when it started to throb. The dull pain was still there, but her sudden bossiness made him smile. She narrowed her stern gaze on him, and he did as she'd ordered.

It wasn't bleeding, he was pretty sure. The bullet had only grazed him, and while she was gone last night he'd used a hand mirror to check out the injury. Considering the doctor's place was as sterile as a back alley, the wound was healing well. He suspected that the sporadic headaches and throbbing had more to do with the banging around that went with the truck rolling.

He didn't even need a bandage anymore, but he said nothing as she stood over him, peeling away the gauze and checking the gash. Her nearness was good enough medicine. He inhaled her flowery feminine scent, his gaze lingering on the creamy skin just above the neckline of her dress. She'd gone to sleep in the same green dress she'd been wearing after returning from her bath. Like the blue one, it was too big on her, with a tendency to slip down her shoulder.

She wasn't wearing a bra, or a corset, or whatever it was that women wore under their dresses in the 1800s. Not that he could tell, anyway. She was fairly small-chested, slight in every way, except her arms were strong and toned, and she wasn't soft-looking like Kitty or the other woman, Lola, at whom he'd gotten a fairly good look yesterday.

Come to think of it, Rebecca tended to have a modern woman's body, like someone who did yoga or light weight training. He noticed too that the backs of her hands were tan, as was her face, at odds with the paleness of the skin around her neckline. Odd, because it was too cold for much outdoor activity. But she'd told him she'd only been here two weeks. Maybe she'd been traveling. Probably by covered wagon. The thought boggled his mind.

She turned away for a second to grab a small pouch off the stool, giving him a good view of her backside. For being so slender, her rear was nice and round, and he was pretty sure there wasn't any type of undergarment giving that illusion. When she faced him again, he instantly lifted his gaze, surprised to see his guilt reflected in her eyes.

Which made him suspicious of the small buckskin pouch. He'd be damned if he'd drink or take anything again. "What's in there?"

She let out a huffing breath of air that seemed so uncharacteristic of her it took him aback. "It's medicine. Good medicine."

"Nothing is going in this mouth. You got it?"

Her lips twitched, and then she lifted her chin. "It is not supposed to go into your mouth."

"Good." He eyed the pouch. "What's in there?"

"Medicine."

"You said that. Be more specific."

She frowned. "It's to help you heal."

"You put it here," he asked, lightly probing the side of his head.

Rebecca nodded. "And here." She used her thumb to touch the corner of his mouth where a blister had been, and then promptly drew back.

He had to admit, whatever salve she'd been applying had done the trick on his lips. Two days ago the blisters had been so bad it hurt to drink. "May I see it?"

She quickly uncoiled a string attached to the pouch. "You don't need any more. You're healing fine," she said, looping the string around her neck and tucking the pouch into her neckline.

"Well, darlin', now I'm really curious."

Very businesslike, she collected the old bandage and tape. "Doc Davis will be by later to look at this. We'll wait to see if he thinks you need another bandage."

"You know, I think I could use a little more of that medicine on my lips." He made a show of probing the one spot on the outside corner that wasn't quite back to normal.

She narrowed her eyes in suspicion. "It looks very good to me."

"Stings a bit, though."

She hesitated, before drawing out the pouch. Then she went to the basin, giving him her back, while she ostensibly washed her hands. But he knew better…she didn't want him seeing what was in the pouch. It took him a few seconds to decide if he wanted to force the issue, just long enough for her to produce the mystery salve on the tip of her finger without him seeing the source.

He smiled, and lifted his chin for her ministration. At the last moment, before she applied it to his mouth, he caught her wrist and peered at the thick white milky substance.

It had no odor, but there was something familiar about the consistency. He frowned, digging deep to remember where he'd seen it. "Ah." He nodded. "Cactus sap, right?"

She looked startled at first, and then fear filled her eyes and she pulled away from him.

"Go ahead," he said, pointing to his mouth. "You're right. This is good stuff. Great for sunburns." He added wryly, "Stove burns, too."

She didn't move, just stared at him as if she thought he were mocking her.

"My grandmother used something similar to this. She actually grew some in her greenhouse." He smiled, acknowledging that Rebecca had no idea what a greenhouse was. "My point is, you're right. It's good medicine."

"Truly?"

He took a dab off her finger and spread it on the blistered area. "It's been working, hasn't it?"

Rebecca smiled, so big that her left cheek dimpled, and then she sobered. "Doc Davis doesn't like me to use the sap. He calls it heathen medicine."

Jake snorted. Doc Davis had a whole shelf of so-called remedies that would be crucified in the journals of medicine in the future. But he wouldn't be around to know that. And most likely, neither would Jake.

The reminder of his bizarre circumstances depressed him. Was he destined to return? How did this whole thing work? If his fate was to change the history of the Rangers, then once his mission was completed did he get to return to the future? If so, how?

Or would time forget about him. Leave him here to live out the rest of his days.

"Your grandmother, where does she live?" Rebecca asked.

"She died about eight years ago."

"I'm sorry."

"And your folks?"

She looked stricken, and then agitated that she'd brought up the subject. "My parents and brother, they've been gone about five years now."

"I'm sure it's been tough."

She gave a small shrug and, instead of returning the pouch to the safety of her bodice, she tucked it once again next to the basin. The sign of trust touched him.

"I'll put up some coffee and then go check with Cook about breakfast."

"Want me to come with you? No sense you carrying the food all the way up here."

She shook her head, pressing a hand to her stomach. "It's not good for the Rangers to see you."

Damn, he hated to see the fear storm her face every time she spoke of the Rangers. He sure as hell didn't look forward to admitting that he was a Ranger. She wouldn't understand, and she'd likely lump him with the rest of those poor excuses for lawmen.

"I take it they don't know I'm staying here." He was going to have to meet these men for himself soon. He hoped they weren't all like that filth Corbin.

"They do. Kitty made it all right with Captain Wade. She told him you were too sick to be turned out."

"Ah. He won't share that opinion once he sees me."

She studied him for a second. "You don't have a horse or gun or money. You'll have to find work."

Jake nodded grimly. "Yep. That's about the only thing I know for certain."

"The Rangers…they'll ask you to work for them." She didn't seem the least bit happy about that prospect.

"Doing what?"

Pressing her lips together, as if she feared she'd said too much, she hesitated. "I'll get your breakfast."

"Bring some for yourself, too. And don't tell me you've already eaten. I know better." He caught the defiant toss of her hair before she left the room, and smiled. Yeah, he had some nerve ordering her to do anything, but she didn't eat enough. She was too thin and he'd even wondered if she'd been on some kind of hunger strike.

He'd resorted to blackmail last night, refusing to eat the beans and cornbread unless she ate with him. She'd picked at her food, using her fingers to tear off small morsels of the cornbread and taking too long to chew and swallow. It occurred to him that she herself might be sick, yet she'd proven to be strong, and if that were the case, he doubted Kitty, who seemed protective of Rebecca, would have burdened her with caring for him.

Man, he had so many questions. About the rustling and hangings, about what the hell a bunch of Rangers were doing to instill fear in the townspeople, about Rebecca and why she was here. And damn, he needed to talk to Slow Jim. He hoped like hell the guy remembered exactly where he'd found Jake. That piece of information could be his only clue to get home.

There was no getting around it. Rebecca obviously wasn't going to be happy about his decision. But Jake knew it was time for him to start circulating.

REBECCA KEPT HER HEAD DOWN as she moved through the quiet saloon to the safety of the kitchen. Not a soul was in sight. Not even the occasional drunk who'd passed out and was left with his head lying on a table. Seven of the Rangers had ridden out a couple of hours before sunup. She'd known from Kitty that they were leaving, so she'd listened for them from the bed she'd made on the floor.

The two men who'd remained were likely still asleep, or maybe even drunk.

Cook was stooped over a large black iron pot, his back to her when she entered the kitchen.

"Morning," Rebecca said loudly so she wouldn't startle the older man.

He couldn't hear in one ear, and only some in the other. Even now, he straightened his rounded shoulders, and stopped stirring as if wondering if he'd heard something.

"Good morning, Cook," Rebecca repeated.

He twisted around and gave her a big grin. Most of his teeth were missing, and what were left were horribly yellow. A pair of ugly scars slashed across his left cheek and his gray hair was so wiry it stuck out everywhere. He'd nearly scared her to death the first time she'd met him, but Cook had turned out to be a very nice man.

"You gonna be wantin' some ham and eggs this mornin'?" he asked with a sly wink.

She understood him completely. When Captain Wade was gone, the girls got to have more than biscuits and porridge for breakfast. "Yes," she said, smiling. "I'd like a plate for my patient."

"Plenty enough for you, too, girly," he said with a stern frown, and waving of his long-handled spoon. "It'll be ready in ten minutes."

She nodded her thanks, and hid her annoyance. Why was everyone worried about how much she ate? She supposed she should be more tolerant. No one understood how her life had been for the past five years. Cold nomadic winters, the scarcity of nuts and berries. Warriors and children ate first. Women made do with what was left. Rebecca had learned to exist on very little. Food wasn't a problem now, there was always plenty here in Diablo Flats, but sometimes the diet she'd been accustomed to as a child living back East no longer agreed with her sensitive belly.

She left the kitchen and hurried over to Doc Davis's while Cook made their breakfast. Doc had told her it would be all right to take the book she'd been reading while she'd sat with Jake those two nights. She liked to read and was quite good at it. As a girl she'd always loved going to school and even thought she might want to teach one day. But that was a long time ago. Before she and her family had started out west. Before that wretched summer night five years ago....

Oh, God, she had to stop herself from thinking about it or she'd be depressed for the rest of the week. She hesitated outside Doc's door, squeezing her eyes shut, forcing the black thoughts from her mind. Instead, she went to the sunny place she'd learned to paint inside her head, with the clear blue skies and puffy clouds and colorful rainbows.

Doc wasn't around when she entered the sickroom. Mr. Otis was still lying face up, eyes closed, still as a rock, just like he'd been when she and Jake had left yesterday. Her heart ached at the sight of him, his throat still an ugly red. No one believed he'd broken the law, yet here he was, inches from death, according to Kitty.

Rebecca glanced toward the door that led to Doc Davis's living quarters to make sure it was closed. Her hand went for the pouch around her neck. It wasn't there. Panic hit her, and then she remembered she'd left the cactus sap with Jake. Funny, because she rarely left the pouch off her person. But Jake had surprised her. He hadn't scolded her, like the doctor had, or made fun of her like Ruby and Lola had done. Jake accepted that the sap was good medicine, and that made her like him even more.

Her fingers went to her lips, and she lightly touched the spot where he'd pressed his mouth to hers. Simply thinking about the soft kiss brought a warmth to her chest that gushed like a swollen river to her belly. The unexpected surge of heat took her by surprise. She bit down on her lip, hard, shame demanding the punishing bite. She had no right to yearn for another man's touch. To dishonor her husband this way was unforgivable.

8

JAKE HATED the tense silence that had accompanied their breakfast. As usual, Rebecca ate very little, only a small portion of the eggs and a biscuit. When she'd slid her slice of ham onto his plate, he'd tried to refuse, but in the end, he knew she wouldn't eat it and he was still hungry. That's how he knew for sure he was recovering well. His appetite had returned full force.

"Thanks for making breakfast," he said while he gathered their utensils and cloth napkins, and stacked their plates.

She eyed him as if he'd done something unspeakable. "I'll take those," she said, scrambling to her feet.

"I can wash them. Do we have dish soap?"

She stared at him with blatant curiosity. "Washing is women's work."

He laughed. "Ah, there's a lot to be said for the good old days."

Not even a hint of a smile touched the corners of her mouth as she took the plates from him, carefully, almost as if she were trying not to touch his fingers.

"Cook made our breakfast, so I'll thank him for you,"

she murmured, her eyes downcast. "Ruby, Trixie and I take turns washing dishes."

"I can help."

"No." She adamantly shook her head.

He sighed, not so anxious to pitch in, but feeling cooped up. Another sign he was feeling better. "How long have I been here in Diablo Flats?"

She thought for a second. "Almost five days." Then she made a face.

"What?" He followed her gaze, looking down at his shirt, the one she'd altered for him.

"It's too small."

He tugged at the cuffs that were a half inch too short even with the piece of material she'd added. So was the hem, but it wouldn't be noticeable once he tucked it in.

"Kitty is getting me fabric. I'll start sewing your new shirt this afternoon."

"This is fine." He unsnapped his jeans and drew down the zipper.

Rebecca gasped. Her eyes widened in shock, and then she spun around to avert her reddening face.

"Hey, no." He quickly tucked in his shirttails, snapped and zipped. "Rebecca." He cupped his hands over her shoulders, feeling her tense. "I was just tucking my shirt into my waistband."

"Oh." Her shoulders seemed to melt beneath his palms.

"You can turn around," he said, and lightly squeezed, struck again at how fragile she felt. It wasn't just that she was so slender, but she had really tiny bones.

Is that what stirred his protective instinct? Even as drugged and weak as he'd been the day Corbin had shown up, Jake had been ready to drag himself out of bed and pound the guy to a bloody pulp. Naturally he never liked seeing a woman abused physically or verbally, but his re-action had been magnified that day yet he'd barely known Rebecca.

She hesitated, and he had to give her a gentle nudge to face him again. Her cheeks were still pink, and it finally dawned on him that in her line of work, a man taking off his clothes shouldn't faze her.

"I'm sorry," she murmured. "I shouldn't have thought you would—" She gave her head a shake, and backed away.

"How long have you been doing this?"

Her brows drew together in a puzzled frown.

"Doing the kind of work you do," he said, wishing he knew a gentler way to ask, and then wincing inwardly as shame filled her eyes.

She immediately stared down at the floor. "I haven't done it yet," she said softly, her voice a thread below a whisper.

"What do you mean?"

She hugged her ribs tightly with one hand, bending for-ward slightly.

"Rebecca." He felt like crap for pushing but he had to know. "What did you do before you came to Diablo Flats?"

"Please, I have to go. Cook must be waiting for me."

He caught her hand, and then urged her chin up until she met his eyes. "I know you don't have to talk to me. None of this is my business. But you don't belong here, Rebecca. Anyone can see that."

That she looked so sad and helpless tore at his insides. "I haven't done it," she repeated.

"You mean, been with a man?" he asked, ducking his head because she'd lowered her eyelids.

She hesitated, catching her lip with her even white teeth, biting down so hard he saw a speck of blood.

"Hey." Damn, what an insensitive bastard he was being. What the hell was wrong with him? "Stop." He brushed the pad of his thumb across her lip. "It doesn't matter. I'm sorry."

"I haven't brought a man upstairs yet," she murmured, moving her head back enough to break contact. He got the message and lowered his hand. "Kitty makes sure of it. She sends me to help Doc Davis." She blinked. "But soon the railroad men are coming and the whole town will be busy and she doesn't know if—" She shrugged her slim shoulders.

Anger erupted hotly inside him. "You never have to bring a man up here. Do you understand?"

"But the Rangers said—"

"I don't give a damn what they said."

She shrank back, her unblinking eyes round and wary.

"I'm not yelling at you. I'm just frustrated. I want to help you, but right now I don't see how." Damn, that was hard for him to admit. Maybe learning humility was supposed to be his lesson in this journey. He hoped not. He didn't do humility well. "You said something about the Rangers having work for me."

Rebecca stepped further back, adamantly shaking her head, her face flushed with a fierce protectiveness that startled him. "Jake, no."

Had he heard her use his name before? He didn't think so. "I know you don't like the idea," he said, moving closer and running his palm up her arm. "I don't either, but the truth is, without money and a horse, I can't help get you out of here."

"You want to help me?" she whispered.

"Of course I do. This is no place for you." He kept

rubbing her arm, pleased that she hadn't withdrawn from him.

"I don't know." She looked torn. Hope lit her eyes, but only for a second before fear extinguished it. "I want to leave. I do. But these are very bad men."

"I promise you, I can take care of myself." Hell, with his bruised ribs still healing, he was going to have to watch his temper and not get into a brawl. He wasn't hotheaded like he'd been when he was younger. Ironically, being a Ranger had knocked some of the arrogance out of him. The behavior wasn't tolerated. But this was a different time, and he suspected posturing and fists were often used in place of reasoning.

She shook her head. "They could hurt you if you get in their way."

"Or worse, they'll hurt you, and I can't stand by and watch that happen." Jake opened his arms to her. She had to come to him this time, of her own free will, showing she trusted him.

Rebecca's chin quivered. She looked as if she desperately wanted to believe he'd help her, but she couldn't quite make that leap. He was about to drop his arms to his side, when she rushed toward him, throwing her arms around his middle.

He gritted his teeth against the sudden pain. She'd obviously forgotten about his ribs, and no way would he let on that she'd nearly made him cry like a damn baby. He hugged her to his chest, and her arms lowered to his waist where they did less damage.

She tilted her head back to gaze at him with glassy eyes. "I'll bring you trouble," she said softly. "Once you leave this room, you have to stay far away from me."

He touched her cheek. "That's not going to happen."

"Please, Jake." She pressed against him, her shoulder digging in right where it hurt.

He must have reacted without realizing it, because she gasped and abruptly drew back with a look of horror.

"I'm sorry."

"No," he said, "don't." He caught her around her waist and brought her back to him, but this time slowly and carefully. "I like feeling you close to me."

"Your side…"

"Just don't whack me."

She smiled a little, and then sighed. "I like feeling you close to me, too."

Jake kissed the top of her head, and then the tip of her nose. Both very chaste kisses, neither of which, along with the residual throb at his side, stopped him from getting hard. He hoped she wasn't pressed close enough to feel his arousal. She was being careful keeping adequate distance not to hurt him so he didn't think she could. The last thing he wanted to do was scare her off.

She stared up at him, her fathomless blue-green eyes fixed on his mouth, and then she raised herself on tiptoe. He lowered his head to meet her part way, but waited for her to make the final move. The decision clearly didn't come easy for her, but she touched her lips to his, the slight tremor that shook her body getting to him in a way he didn't understand, rousing emotions that he refused to examine.

The sweet taste of her was all he wanted or needed. It didn't even matter that the kiss was brief. He still didn't know if she completely trusted him, but Rebecca steadfastly didn't want to see him hurt. And for now, that was enough.

"CAPTAIN WADE WILL be returning in time for supper," Kitty told the girls as she set up trays at the end of the bar.

"So make sure y'all have had at least two customers by then and everyone else in the place is drinking steady."

Lola rolled her dark kohl-lined eyes. "Two customers." She snorted and patted her black upswept hair. She wore two red feathers that matched her dress. Rebecca thought they looked silly but she would never say so, especially not to Lola, who sometimes threw glasses and bottles when she was in a temper. "By supper I will have five customers begging for seconds."

Trixie laughed. With a look of disgust, Ruby pulled a slim cigar from her bodice and walked toward the porch for a smoke. Lola went in the other direction, toward the only two customers in the saloon. The men had been drinking for most of the afternoon and were slumped over their table.

Rebecca knew Ruby and Lola didn't always get along. Both women had mostly ignored her since she'd arrived, and she was happy to stay out of their way. Trixie had been more friendly, but right now, Rebecca wanted to talk to Kitty alone. In another hour she wouldn't have a chance. The saloon would be too crowded.

Almost as if Kitty sensed Rebecca's need to talk, she asked Trixie to check with Cook about having Captain Wade's supper ready before he arrived. Rebecca waited until Trixie was out of sight, and then said, "Jake says he's coming downstairs after he cleans up. He wants to work for the Rangers."

"Good."

Rebecca reared her head back. "How can you say such a thing?"

Kitty sniffed the clean glasses the bartender had set near the trays, and then nodded her approval. "The man needs a horse and gun, and he needs to make money. Better to be Wade's friend than his enemy."

"Jake can find work on a ranch away from town." Rebecca didn't try to hide her disappointment in Kitty. The woman had been her friend from the beginning. When Rebecca had tried to steal a horse and knife the day after she'd been brought to town, it was Kitty who convinced her the timing was wrong to try and escape.

"Look, honey." Kitty glanced around and pulled Rebecca away from the bar and the bartender's big ears. "You'd have to be blind to miss seein' that Jake isn't an average fella. He's too smart and quick. He's no cowhand, that's for sure. Besides, you really think he'll go hole up on some ranch and leave you here in town with these miserable coyotes?"

Rebecca felt the heat climb her throat, and wondered what Kitty had seen or heard to make her think Jake would care that much about her.

Kitty chuckled. "Don't go getting embarrassed. It's plain as day that he cares for you. I wish I had a man like that to run to." Kitty sobered, and lowered her voice. "Does he know?"

She drew in a deep breath. No need to ask if Kitty was talking about the past five years. Rebecca's captivity was no secret around here. At least not among the Rangers. She suspected that Cook and Lloyd, the bartender, also knew. But they wouldn't say anything for fear of Captain Wade. Word got out, and men wouldn't pay to sleep with an Indian whore. She'd heard the hateful words often enough, but thinking about them still had the power to slice through her. "I haven't told him."

"You fixing to?"

"I don't know." She knew that was a lie. He'd kissed her. She'd kissed him back. He had a right to know. But he'd likely hate her, and she couldn't bear that thought right now.

"He might not be the sort who cares about such a thing," Kitty said, quickly glancing away, telling Rebecca that she didn't believe her own words.

Her heart heavy, Rebecca stared down at the floor. Maybe tonight she'd take a horse and knife and leave this place. Even if she were caught, let them hang her. Her life was over anyway.

"I wouldn't be hasty telling him anything." Kitty touched her arm. "He's your chance to get out of here. You took good care of him over at Doc Davis's. Let Jake take on work and make enough money to get you out of Texas. That's what I'd call evening things up. Your past can stay right where it is."

Rebecca truly wished that could be so without feeling empty inside. She didn't like to lie, especially not to Jake. Or to Kitty. She'd be horrified to know that Rebecca had no intention of leaving Texas. The only other two people who'd treated her with such kindness in the past year were Bird Song and Meadow Flower. She missed the two women who'd been like a mother and sister to her, and Kitty wouldn't understand…she might even hate Rebecca for wanting to return to the tribe. She didn't simply *want* to return. She had to. After learning what she had from Doc Davis's books, Rebecca owed it to Bird Song to find her.

"I've got to get back to work," Kitty said. "When Jake comes down, don't be too chummy with him around the saloon. It might set Corbin off."

At the mention of his name, Rebecca shuddered. She wasn't sure she understood that remark, but Kitty had already returned to the bar, where Lloyd waited with another tray of glasses for Kitty to dry and stack in preparation for the busy night.

Her gaze going to the stairs, Rebecca sidled up next to

Kitty and picked up a rag to help her with the drying. She figured that by the time Jake had shaved and washed, he'd be coming down about now. Although he wasn't like the other men around town. He took bathing seriously. She smiled to herself thinking about his frustration over using only a basin to wash. She told him about the bathhouse, but he didn't have money and he refused to borrow any from Kitty.

Instead, he'd asked for extra water and warned her that he might make a mess on the floor. He'd also promised to clean it up himself. He was a puzzle, for sure. In her experience, men, no matter what color, never cleaned up after themselves. And they certainly weren't worried about being so clean. She liked that about Jake a lot.

She wondered suddenly about what he'd look like shaved. Dark stubble had covered his face from the first day Slow Jim had brought him to town. He'd be even more handsome, she was sure of it. Sighing, she picked up another wet glass. It slipped from her hand, hit the floor and shattered. Shards of glass flew everywhere.

"Goddamn it." The bartender leaned over the bar to peer at the scattered pieces, and then glared at Rebecca. "Ain't you good for anything around here?"

Rebecca swallowed, and dropped to the floor to clean up the broken glass.

"Shut up, Lloyd." Kitty glared back at him, ignoring Rebecca's pleading eyes. She didn't want Kitty to get in trouble because of her. "You got time to be jawing, you got time to dry your own damn glasses."

"Watch your mouth, you stupid whore. You don't scare me none just because—"

One brow arched up. "Yes?" Kitty said, leaning across the bar toward Lloyd, her voice deadly calm.

The bartender backed up. "I'll get the broom. That best be cleaned up before the next customer comes in."

Rebecca pressed her lips together to keep from smiling at the look on Lloyd's face. She'd heard the tittle-tattle about Kitty the second day she was here. The story went that a man had beaten her up once, and she cut off his private parts in his sleep. Lola claimed it was a rumor, but Ruby and Trixie swore the story was true.

Rebecca stood to take the broom from Lloyd, and forced herself to meet his small hateful black eyes. For a second, she wished she were already across the street, sitting with Mr. Otis while Doc Davis made his evening calls. She would've been there if she hadn't been waiting for Jake to come down. But she was also tired of being bullied by these men.

"Indian whore," he mouthed silently.

"Go to hell, Lloyd." It was Kitty, who'd apparently seen him. "Heard they have a special place waiting down there for you." She tugged at Rebecca's sleeve.

But Rebecca wouldn't look away. She wasn't sure what had gotten into her, but she refused to let him stare her down. It helped that in her hand, she'd secreted a nice long shard of glass. She wouldn't use it, didn't even know if she were capable, but she was so tired of these awful men....

"Good evening, ladies."

Jake's voice snapped her out of her trance. She turned sharply toward him.

"Is there a problem?" he asked calmly, his eyes glittering dangerously.

9

"No." Rebecca squeezed the broom handle, trying not to wince when the glass bit into her palm. Heaven help her, had he seen what Lloyd had mouthed to her? Is that why he'd seemed angry? She started to look away, afraid of what she might see if she stared too long, but then Jake turned his attention to the bartender.

"Everything is just peachy," Kitty said with a sassy smile. "Right, Lloyd?"

The bartender snarled. "The girls said you were sick. You look fine to me."

"Almost good as new." His chin and cheeks were smooth, the dimple in his chin deeper than she thought, and his long dark hair freshly washed. He looked so handsome she nearly ached from just setting eyes on him.

"Then you ain't got no business staying up there." The bartender cocked his head toward the balcony. "Better get your ass out in the street."

Jake looked at him with a mildly amused expression on his face. "You must be Captain Wade."

"What?" Lloyd seemed confused. "No."

"My mistake. Though you can't blame me, what with

you strutting your feathers and pretending to be the big boss," Jake said with a taunting curve of his mouth.

Kitty hooted with laughter.

"Why, you goddamn—" Lloyd reached under the bar where he kept his shotgun.

Rebecca opened her mouth to warn Jake, but with lightning speed, he lurched across the oak bar and grabbed the front of Lloyd's shirt. The bartender shrieked, his eyes bulging as Jake yanked him forward across the bar, inches from his face.

"You swore in front of the ladies," Jake said quietly. "And you irritated me. So this is what you're going to do. First, you'll apologize to them, then you'll hand me that gun you were going for, barrel first. After that, you're going to pour each of us a drink on the house. Understand?"

Lloyd's eyes got even bigger, but he stubbornly refused to respond, until Jake jerked again. One of the snaps popped off his shirt.

"You take too long, and that just irritates me further. You really wanna do that, buddy?" Jake didn't look angry anymore. In fact, his features bore no expression at all.

But then Rebecca saw his other hand supporting his injured side. He had to be hurting, pressed up against the bar like he was. God, she prayed Lloyd would just give in.

"I'm reaching for the shotgun now," the bartender muttered, his eyes brimming with hatred.

"Forgetting something?" His eyes fixed on the other man, Jake made a slight gesture with his chin toward her and Kitty.

"I'm sorry," Lloyd ground out through clenched teeth, and then withdrew the shotgun by the barrel and passed it to Jake.

"Thank you." Jake smiled. "Ladies, will you sit with me while you have your drinks?"

Kitty, who seemed as shocked as Rebecca, shook her head. "Sorry, sugar, I've got to get ready for work."

"Rebecca?"

She met his eyes, her heart still pounding. "I promised to go to Doc Davis's and sit with Mr. Otis."

"Another time then." He gave her a small nod like a gentleman would do to a lady, and then reached for her hand. Or was it the broom he wanted?

Panicked, confused, she abruptly moved back, not wanting him to discover the shard of glass she held pressed between the handle and her palm.

"I have to sweep up this glass," she said.

"I know," he said, holding her gaze, and with gentle force, circled his fingers around her wrist to keep her from fleeing.

She held her breath, knowing she was about to die at any second. She wouldn't be able to explain hiding the glass. Lloyd would accuse her of wanting to cut him.

Jake smoothly took the broom from her, and then quickly cupped his hand over the shard of glass so that it was lightly pressed between their two palms. She nearly choked on her tongue when he brought the back of her hand to his lips. He placed a light kiss there, and then withdrew his hand, taking the shard with him.

It happened so fast, him as slick as a seasoned card player that she doubted anyone saw a thing.

Lloyd snorted. "Well, if that don't beat all."

Kitty sighed. "Shut your fat mouth, Lloyd, and put these glasses behind the bar." She started toward the back, but abruptly stopped, her lips parting in surprise as she stared past Rebecca. "Wade, you're early."

Rebecca spun around toward the front of the saloon.

Her insides quaked at the sight of him, his arms resting over the tops of the swinging doors as he peered inside. Captain Wade was a giant of a man, even taller than Jake. He had hard gray eyes, and a humorless face she'd never seen without whiskers.

"I heard a ruckus in here," he said, strolling inside, the heels of his boots thumping the floor, the jingle of his spurs pricking her nerve endings.

His gaze surveyed each face, lingering too long on Jake's, and making Rebecca's stomach roll. Fearing how much he'd seen and heard, she moved closer to Kitty. Her first instinct had been to go to Jake, but she knew that might cause trouble for both of them.

"Nothing, really," Kitty assured him, shrugging. "A glass slipped out of Rebecca's hand, and Lloyd overreacted. You gonna want your supper soon?"

He pulled off his hat and then his gloves, unmindful of the dust that sullied the air, and tossed everything on a nearby table. He didn't answer Kitty, but rather kept his eyes fixed on Jake. "I reckon you're the fella Slow Jim found north of town."

"That's what they tell me." Jake didn't seem the least bit uneasy meeting Captain Wade. With a faint smile, he stuck out his hand. "Name's Jake Malone."

"Wade Gibson."

"That's Captain Gibson to you," Lloyd cut in, eyeing Jake with a smug smile, his arms crossed over his round belly.

"Shut up, and get us a whiskey." Captain Wade exhaled tiredly and stretched his neck to the side, and then without looking at Kitty or Rebecca, growled, "Don't you women have work to do?"

Rebecca promptly resumed her sweeping, but Kitty made a motion with her head, telling Rebecca she should ignore the glass and leave. Any other time, she would've jumped at the chance. But she hated not knowing what would happen between Jake and Captain Wade.

This strange side to Jake bewildered her, filled her with contrary feelings she couldn't readily sort out. He'd been so gentle with her, kind and tender, but he was different now. His face seemed darker, more sharply defined, a subtle shift, but enough to make her nervous, enough to make her wonder what kind of dark secrets lurked in his suddenly emotionless blue eyes.

She hesitated too long, and got another stern look from Kitty. Slowly she headed toward the swinging doors, knowing her friend meant for her to head to Doc Davis's. At the doors, she paused again, unable to resist a last look at Jake. Their eyes met. Just for a moment, and then he winked.

JAKE WISHED HE KNEW how much Wade had seen and heard before making his presence known. The man had an excellent poker face. So did Jake. No matter what, this was going to be interesting. He just didn't want Rebecca involved.

What the hell had she been thinking, hiding that sharp piece of glass? She'd made him nervous, the way she'd stared at the bartender with such intense loathing. Jake didn't think she would've actually used the shard as a weapon, or maybe he simply hoped that she would've shown restraint. What did he really know about her? Except that she was scared out of her mind. And frightened people often did stupid things.

Wade stood at the bar, one boot on the brass rail. He lifted his glass of whiskey, threw his head back, downing the entire shot. Then he set it back down, and indicated to the bartender that he wanted a refill, even though the bottle had been left within his reach. "What brings you to these parts?" he asked Jake, his dark eyes appearing neutral, but the man clearly missed nothing.

"Can't say. I banged my head up pretty good. Don't remember how, or what I was doing here." Jake took a cautious sip of the harsh liquor. "The doctor says it could still come to me."

Wade toyed with his replenished glass. "Not much of a drinking man, I see."

"Sometimes." Jake shrugged. "But like I said, my head is messed up enough."

The other man almost smiled. Instead, he brought the whiskey again to his mouth, but this time sipped slowly. "A wise man knows when to put the bottle down." He pulled over a stool and sat near Jake. "Don't see too much of that around here."

The bartender didn't look happy. He gave Jake a sour look, which made him wonder if he'd just passed some kind of unspoken test. Mostly to annoy the jackass bartender, Jake pulled up a stool, too.

Wade set down his glass, and shrugged out of his coat, made from some kind of animal skin, though not leather. The unexpected dose of reality sent a chill down Jake's spine. He was out of his element and had to watch his speech and mannerisms. Even if he slipped up and they thought he was a city slicker from back East, that could still be bad for him.

He concentrated on his whiskey, his mind racing while Wade got rid of his coat. The other men couldn't be far behind. They'd all be curious, most of them territorial. Having this chance to get to know the head guy was the best scenario Jake could've hoped for.

"You know what's for supper?" Wade asked the bartender. "If you don't, go find out."

Jake turned from his whiskey so he could see Lloyd's

face, but his gaze snagged on the dull silver badge pinned to Wade's shirt. A circle with a star in the middle. Jake barely made out the word *Texas* scratched out at the top of the circle, but it didn't matter. He recognized the old Ranger's badge. The style hadn't changed, only the wording.

Excitement, awe, disbelief all converged inside of him. If he hadn't gotten it that he'd somehow landed back in 1800s Texas, he would have now. This was the real deal. He knew quite a bit about Ranger history. Hell, as a kid he'd been to the museum dozens of times, heard his father and grandfather tell the same stories over and over throughout the years. They not only talked about their own experiences as Rangers, but passed on tales they'd heard as boys.

He picked up his whiskey and finished it off.

Wade pushed the bottle toward him. It was only then that Jake realized the Ranger had been staring at him.

Jake pulled himself together. Later, he'd reminisce, and wrack his brain for any mention of a Captain Wade Gibson from the history books. Right now he had to stay sharp. He picked up the bottle and poured himself half a shot he had no intention of finishing.

"You're still hurt," Wade observed.

Jake didn't know where that had come from. Unless the emotion that had spiraled through him had translated into a look of pain on his face. He decided not to respond.

Wade frowned. "I saw you favor your side when you pulled Lloyd over the bar."

"I'm still healing."

The other man nodded, a hint of admiration in his eyes. "Even banged up, you know how to handle yourself. You stay cool, too. That's good. You hungry?" His gaze shifted toward the back of the saloon, in the direction the bartender had disappeared.

"I could eat."

"Hey, Lloyd," the Ranger yelled. "What the hell are you doing? Killing the goddamn cow?"

The bartender hurried toward them carrying a plate of food. "Cook made chicken and dumplings, boss. Unless you'd rather he fry you up a steak—"

"Give it here." Wade took the plate from him. "Go get another one, and don't be stingy with the chicken," he said, frowning at the thick white goulash before setting it in front of Jake.

Lloyd swore under his breath, loud enough for Jake to hear, but not Wade. "I don't expect there's gonna be enough food for the boys if you aim to start giving away handouts."

"What did you say?" Wade speared the man with a menacing look that stopped him in his tracks. "I don't reckon I took your meaning."

"It was nothing, boss." Lloyd hurried toward the back of the saloon.

Wade chuckled, taking obvious pleasure in belittling the man. "Damn pussy. Good thing for him he keeps a good bar," he said, leaning back, stretching his arms above his head, and yawning. "Sure am looking forward to trading in my bedroll for a bed tonight."

Jake picked up the fork that was sitting on the plate. "I heard you've been busy lately."

"Meaning?" he asked in a suspicious voice.

"Going after those rustlers."

"What would you know about that?"

"Nothing much. I heard the women talking."

Wade snorted. "They got better things to do than yapping about matters that don't concern them." The man eyed Jake with new interest. "Maybe you're one of them rustlers and don't remember."

"Could be," he said, mostly to catch Wade off guard,

which he noticed, was exactly what he did. Jake smiled. He read people well, it was part of his job, and he surmised Wade was the type who needed to be kept guessing. Once he was bored, he'd be likely to throw Jake to the coyotes. "But that doesn't feel right. I'm not a rustler."

"When it comes to making a few quick pieces of silver, a man would do a lot of things."

"True enough." Jake forked a piece of chicken and put it in his mouth. It had turned out to be good luck that Wade had seen the incident with Lloyd. Now Wade knew he wasn't a pussy, as he liked to put it, and he might be guessing that Jake would be willing to hire out muscle. That being the case, the captain might be more forthcoming with what was going on around here.

"I kind of like you, Malone. I'd hate to find out you're on the wrong side of the law." A slow smile spread across his face. "Then I'd have to shoot you."

"Shit."

Wade threw his head back and laughed. "You fast with a gun?"

"Don't know about fast, but I hit what I aim for."

Lloyd returned at that moment with a heaping plate of food that he set in front of Wade. "Anything else, boss?"

"The boys will be in shortly. They're tired and hungry. Make sure their food's hot and ready." Wade twisted around and eyed the two drunks at the corner table, and then scanned the rest of the empty tables. "Where the hell is everybody?"

"It's still early. There'll be a crowd. Don't you fret none." Lloyd threw a towel over his shoulder and slid Jake a look that was more curious than malicious, which made Jake nervous.

Wade shook his head with disgust, and then holding his fork like a shovel, dug into his food. He had to be starving.

In the next three minutes, he barely stopped for air. But he did look up when from behind them, voices rumbled from off the street. A few seconds later the saloon doors creaked open.

"That was quick," he said to the four men who filed in, wearing dusty coats and scuffed boots. "Leon, you'd better have taken care of those horses this time."

The guy with the bulbous nose grunted, his agitated frown going from Jake to the plate in front of him. "They all been watered and getting rubbed down at the livery now."

A shorter man with blond hair and a red handlebar mustache pulled off his gloves. He barely looked at Jake. His gaze went straight up to the balcony where the women stayed, and he smiled.

"Not until you have a bath, Ned. Then you can knock on my door." It was Lola. Jake recognized her accent even before he glanced at the mirror behind the bar and saw the reflection of her leaning over the balcony, wagging a finger at the blond man.

The last two men pulled up stools on the other side of Wade. The one with the long greasy brown hair and sporting a dark beard sniffed his armpit, made a face and then ordered a beer and shot.

"Christ sake, Moses, you gotta stick your nose under there to know you smell like a damn hog?" The ruddy-faced man shook his head in disgust. "Go get a bath before you eat."

"Shut up."

Wade scowled and dropped his fork with a clatter. "All of you shut up. Where's Corbin?"

The two men sitting at the bar shrugged.

At the mention of Corbin's name, Jake tensed. Naturally he knew he'd run into him again at some point. But he wished he could've had more one-on-one time with Wade first.

"Whoever sees him first, you warn him I don't want him getting too drunk to ride." Wade picked up his fork again and resumed eating, ignoring the stares of disgruntled disbelief coming from the men on his right.

Behind them, one of the other men said, "Captain, you don't mean tonight."

Halfway to Wade's mouth, the fork stilled, and he stared menacingly into the mirror behind the bar. The tic at his jaw worked overtime as his eyes found the guy named Ned. Wade didn't say a word. He didn't have to.

Ned looked away as he shrugged out of his coat. Like Wade, he had a badge pinned to his shirt. Jake quickly checked the other three even though he already knew what he'd find. They all wore the star. These disgusting excuses for Rangers—for men. The idea made him sick. But he couldn't allow himself to be distracted. He'd come off as a tough guy, and opened the door to join their ranks. He was in perfect position. There was obvious dissension, which was great timing for him to create discord among them.

Keeping his game face on, he focused on his food. He needed to stay on point, and not let Lloyd or any of the other men get under his skin. Wade was clearly looking for someone with a cool head, tough, smart enough to think for himself and get a job done, yet not challenge Wade's authority. No problem for Jake. If he were careful, and treated this like just another undercover assignment, he could pull this off. Find out what was going on. Intervene if necessary. Maybe change the mottled history of the Rangers.

That overwhelming thought unsettled him. It was more than he could absorb right now. At this point, he had to stay present, and not even think about Rebecca. Because if he did, if he replayed the conflicted expression on her face when he'd bullied the bartender, then he was seriously in danger of screwing the whole thing up.

10

REBECCA PRESSED HER PALM to Mr. Otis's forehead. He felt warm to her. It could be her imagination, or just plain guilt that had her fretting over the man. Doc Davis had stopped in before he left to deliver a baby and told her their patient was doing well, and that he'd even opened his eyes for a short time about an hour ago, but hadn't spoken. Excited over the news, she had immediately put down her book to keep a closer watch in case he opened his eyes again. But her mind kept wandering back to Jake, and what was happening at the saloon.

After changing the cool compress she kept draped over the older man's forehead, she went to the window and peeked outside. It was almost dark, the sun having set an hour ago. This eerie time of the evening was not her favorite. The shadows seemed to play tricks on her eyes, no matter how hard she stared and tried not to blink. Light from the saloon and the hotel helped, though not as much as Rebecca would like.

She started to turn away from the window when she saw someone leave the saloon and cross the street. It looked like Kitty coming toward Doc Davis's but Rebecca held her breath until the figure wrapped in a cloak came closer and she was certain it was her friend.

Kitty opened the door, letting in a blast of frigid air. "Holy Mother of God, it's cold out there." She shivered and pulled her cloak tighter around her body. "If you don't mind, I could use some of that coffee you're heating."

"Is everything all right at the saloon?" Rebecca hurried to fill a cup, her anxious gaze staying on Kitty. She seldom left the saloon once night fell. Too many customers needed drinks and company.

"Everything is fine. Better than fine. Thanks, honey." She wrapped her hands around the warm cup and took a quick sip before adding, "Your Jake has made quite an impression on Wade. The two of them have been sitting at the bar since Wade showed up. Even ate dinner together."

Rebecca frowned, not sure how she felt about that. It was good that Jake wasn't in trouble with Captain Wade for laying his hands on Lloyd, but she still hated that Jake would have anything to do with the Ranger.

"What's that look for?" Kitty gave her a quick frown while on her way to check on Mr. Otis.

She hesitated. Although Kitty had never admitted her fondness for the captain, Rebecca knew they'd known each other for a long time, and she'd seen the yearning in Kitty's eyes. "Are all the Rangers at the saloon?"

"I haven't seen Corbin or Vernon yet. Which suits me just fine." Kitty felt the man's cheek.

"Do you think he has a fever?"

"No, he feels all right. You've got that fire going pretty good. I think that's got him warm. You have any trouble getting some water down his throat?"

Rebecca shook her head. "Doc Davis showed me how to do it real slow. He told me Mr. Otis opened his eyes for a while. I'm hoping he does again."

Kitty smiled, something she didn't do often, and it was a wonder how much younger she seemed. "That's good news. Did he say anything?"

"No. Just made a funny noise. Doc Davis said it'll be a while before he can actually talk with all the damage done to his throat."

"Poor fella." Kitty touched the man's shoulder before turning back to Rebecca. "Now, I reckon you want to hear about your Jake."

She felt the heat sting her cheeks. "He's not my Jake," she murmured.

Kitty chuckled. "I wouldn't put a wager on that one." She took another sip of her coffee, walked over to glance out the window and then turned to Rebecca. "Good that Wade likes him, since he doesn't cotton to most people. I think he'll hire him on before long."

Rebecca forced herself to smile. "He needs work," she said glumly.

"I know how you feel, but don't you see? With the money he makes and the little bit I have saved, he can take you away from here."

Rebecca widened her eyes. Kitty had money saved? Captain Wade wouldn't like that. "Why don't you leave?"

Kitty sighed, her gaze drifting off to someplace in her mind that was hers alone. "I can't."

"Why not?"

"It's too late for me, honey. Whoring is all I know. I've been doing it since I was fifteen."

A sadness weighed Rebecca's heart. Not only because of what Kitty said, but because she'd plainly given up. "What if you go someplace where no one knows you?"

She shrugged. "No matter where I went, no man would want me. I'd be considered an old maid and end up spreading my legs like I've always done. Better the devil you know, my mama used to say." Kitty patted her arm. "Wade ain't so bad when we're alone. I wouldn't have been able to keep you away from the men for as long as I have if not for him. He lets me have my way from time to time."

Her words did not make Rebecca feel any better. How could she ever repay this woman's kindness?

Kitty pressed her red-painted lips together. "But once the railroad men start coming…" She shook her head. "Unless Doc Davis needs you, it won't be easy."

Rebecca shuddered. "I won't be here," she vowed aloud. "I'll steal a horse if I have to."

"It won't come to that, honey. My money's on Jake. He'll take care of you. He's a good man." She pressed a hand to her belly. "I know it right here." She glanced at Mr. Otis, and then toward the window. "I'd better be getting back and tell everyone the good news about Otis. You let me know if he wakes up again."

Rebecca went to get the door, while Kitty wrapped the cloak tighter around herself, making sure the hood covered her ears and hair. She gave a nod, and Rebecca opened the door, flinching at the icy wind that slapped her face. January was usually cold but this was awful. The thought of taking a horse and riding in this weather gave her a chill. But knowing what would happen if she stayed made her want to weep.

After going to the window and watching Kitty slip safely through the saloon doors, Rebecca went to warm her hands at the fire. There was no choice for her. As much as she trusted Kitty's judgment, there was no way to know if Jake would help her, or if he could even be trusted. If he had gained Captain Wade's favor, would he want to leave Diablo Flats? If he did, and took her with him, would he end up feeling burdened by her? Would a taste of the money Captain Wade sometimes threw around change Jake?

A depressing thought suddenly struck her. She abandoned the fire and sought the stool in case her legs gave way. Had they told Jake the truth about her? If they were drinking and were friendly-like, any one of the men could have warned him about her. Feeling sick to her stomach, she bent over, praying the nausea would pass.

She was so caught up in her misery, she almost didn't hear the soft moan. Didn't know if she'd heard anything for sure. She straightened, and stared at Mr. Otis. Although his lips didn't move, she heard the sound again, a quiet moan that had to be coming from him.

And then he slowly moved his head, and opened his eyes.

She swallowed hard, and pushed to her feet. "Mr. Otis?"

His eyes drifted closed, but only for a second and then he stared right at her, fear flickering before his lids lowered again.

"I'll get you some water." She wished Kitty were still here. He'd recognize her and not be afraid.

His lips parted, the movement painfully slow, as if he wanted to speak. Another low moan was all that came out.

"My name is Rebecca," she said, bringing him the cup. "Doc Davis isn't here right now, but you're in his sickroom. How about some water?"

He turned his head away and stared at the wall.

She knew he had to drink. It had been hard trickling water into his mouth, slowly, so that he wouldn't choke. Doc Davis had told her that if he came to, it was real important to get him to drink as much as he was able to swallow on his own.

"Mr. Otis?"

The man stubbornly refused to look at her.

She set down the cup, knowing what she had to do. "Mr. Otis, I'll be right back," she said, as she lifted her shawl from the coat rack. "I'm going to run over to the saloon and get Kitty. You know Kitty, right? She was here a few minutes ago. Maybe you heard her voice?"

He seemed to relax a bit, but she decided not to force him to drink. Kitty had asked her to report if he woke up again, and Rebecca would feel better having her friend here to help. She wrapped her shawl around her shoulders, assured him she wouldn't be long, opened the door and shivered when the chilly air hit her. She truly wished she had a warm coat. Trixie was closest to her size and she'd been kind enough about sharing her clothes, but she hadn't had a coat to spare. It wasn't a problem now, not when she went outside only to run back and forth between Doc's and the saloon, but when the time came for her to ride away from here, without a coat, she'd end up freezing to death within a few hours.

The thought made her shiver again as she paused outside the door and looked up and down the street. For a second, she thought she saw someone slip down the alley next to Doc Davis's living quarters, but decided it had to be her imagination. The only one who used the alley was the doctor and he was miles away by now. Only one couple appeared to have braved this frigid bleak evening, and they were about to enter Isabella's boardinghouse at the far end of town.

She pulled the wool shawl tighter around her shoulders and kept her face down from the sudden brisk wind as she hurried across the street. Loud laughter and piano music spilled out from the saloon, but she hoped it was early enough that the men weren't too drunk yet. All she needed to do was get Kitty's attention. Jake would be there, too. He'd help if she needed him.

Drawing in a deep punishing breath, she pulled the icy air into her lungs. She didn't know Jake, she reminded herself, not really. What she did know for sure was that there was more than one side to a man, not all of it good. Jake was no different. She had to stop looking to him to rescue her. If she were to survive, she needed to rely on herself.

Lifting her chin, she pushed the doors open. With so much noise, no one heard the hinges squeak. The place was as crowded as she'd ever seen it, with men playing cards or drinking and talking at tables. Ruby was easy to spot with the tall blue feather sticking out of her hair, but Kitty was nowhere in sight.

Hoping to spot Kitty's red hair, Rebecca scanned the men at the bar, and saw Jake. He was sitting with Captain Wade, who said something that made Jake laugh. The scene left her heartsick. How could he keep company with the likes of the Rangers? How easily he seemed to become one of them. His behavior only proved to her that men were thorny creatures, sweet one minute, and prickly the next.

Anxious that she couldn't find Kitty, she stepped tentatively into the room. The smell of liquor and sweat made her stomach turn. At the end of the bar she saw Trixie with her arms draped around a tall thin man. If Rebecca could get her attention, she could at least leave word for Kitty.

Clutching her shawl to her breasts, she lowered her head to avoid eye contact with anyone, and hurried toward Trixie.

"Well, looky here." A man as big as an oak tree blocked her way. "Ain't seen you before. I like yeller-haired women."

His arm snaked out and he clamped his hand hard around her wrist. "Let me buy you a whiskey, little darlin.'"

Rebecca gasped. "No, thank you."

He laughed, his foul breath nearly suffocating her. "I got me a shy one."

"Please." She twisted her hand but his grip was too tight. "I have to see Kitty."

"You come with me, and we'll find Kitty together." He laughed, along with a group of men sitting at the bar.

"Come on, Ralph." Trixie sidled up to him, pursed her lips temptingly and placed a hand on his arm. "Let her go. She's busy tending to Otis at Doc's place."

He shook her off. "Mind your own damn business."

"Yeah, Ralph, come on. Let her go."

Rebecca's heart did a flip.

It was Jake, right next to her, his mouth curved in a faint smile, that deadly glint in his eyes that she'd seen earlier focused unblinkingly on the other man. The two of them stared at each other for several seconds, and then the man named Ralph released her.

"Come here, Trixie," he said, hooking his beefy arm around her shoulders before steering her toward the stairs.

"You ought not interfere with the customers and the whores," one of the Rangers sitting at the bar warned Jake under his breath. "Unless you're aiming to make Wade spitting mad."

Jake shrugged, his gaze on Rebecca's face. "You have news about Otis?"

She'd almost forgotten why she'd come. "Yes, he's awake."

"Is he talking yet?" Jake asked.

"No, not to me. That's why I want Kitty to come."

"Kitty?" Jake's voice rose over the crowd. "Anybody know where Kitty is?"

Feeling calmer now with Jake so near, Rebecca skimmed the nameless faces, until her gaze locked with Captain

Wade's. He'd swung toward them, his back to the bar, and he was staring right at her. Another Ranger whispered something in his ear. Captain Wade gave a small nod, as he slowly, purposefully shifted his attention to Jake, his mouth curving in a crafty grin. She felt sick. Not for herself. She would leave this place, no matter what it took, but she didn't want to cause trouble for Jake.

"I think she's in the back." It was Ruby. "I'll go get her."

Rebecca expected the captain to stop Ruby, but he didn't say a word. Just lifted the whiskey to his lips and tossed his head back.

"I'll go sit with Mr. Otis and wait for Kitty," Rebecca murmured, shrinking back toward the door.

Jake pressed a hand to the small of her back. "I'll go with you."

"You can't."

"Why not?"

She glanced toward Captain Wade, glad that she could no longer see his face. "He won't like it."

"Tough. Let's go."

They stepped out into the cold, and though Jake had no coat himself, he drew a protective arm around her shoulders and pulled her close. By the time they got to the sickroom door, Kitty had run out of the saloon with only a shawl.

She came in right behind them, and rushed past Rebecca to Mr. Otis's bedside. Gasping, she jumped back.

"Kitty? What?" Rebecca pressed closer to the older man.

He lay just as she'd left him, except now, with his sightless eyes focused on the ceiling.

"He's dead," Kitty whispered.

"No. He can't be. I was only gone for a few minutes. He was awake. He was trying to talk." Horrified, Rebecca stared at the man. His lips were parted as if he'd been try-ing to say something, as if he'd screamed for help. "This is my fault. I shouldn't have left him." She covered her face with her hands, choking back a sob.

Jake put his arms around her and rubbed her back. "It's not your fault."

The tears came then. She felt so safe and comforted against his broad solid chest, something she hadn't felt in a very long time. But she had no right. She'd been careless, and now a man was dead.

OVER REBECCA'S HEAD, Jake met Kitty's speculative eyes. He had a feeling she was thinking the same thing he was. Otis Sanford had been murdered.

Jake hugged Rebecca tighter, held her for a moment longer, before setting her back. Her face was red, her cheeks damp, and she blinked rapidly trying to stop the tears. Shame flickered in her eyes before she averted them. He caught her chin and brought her face back to his.

"Listen to me. This is not your fault," he said sternly. "Do you understand?"

She sniffed. "It is."

"No." He shook his head, and gestured for Kitty to step aside. "Do you mind?"

Kitty lifted the hem of her voluminous satin skirt and moved back, solemnly glancing from Jake to Otis. His gut told him that she knew there had been foul play, although why she would follow that line of thinking he had no clue. His suspicion was based on years of experience as a law-man, and what modern medicine had taught him.

Aware that both women watched his every move, he lifted one of Otis's eyelids. Petechial hemorrhaging was evident but that would've occurred during the hanging. He closed the man's eyes, and then checked his hands. There was skin and fresh blood under his fingernails.

"When he came to, did he struggle with you?" he asked Rebecca, while giving her a cursory once-over and seeing no marks on her exposed skin.

"No. He didn't want to drink any water, but he just turned his face to the wall."

Kitty moved closer and peered at Otis's hand. "What are you looking at?"

Jake hesitated, not sure what it would accomplish letting the women know his suspicions. Then, too, he didn't want Kitty running to Wade with the information. But Jake couldn't let Rebecca believe the man's death was her fault.

"See this?" He indicated the tissue and blood under the nails. "Looks as if someone attacked him, and he tried to fight them off."

The women frowned at the evidence, and then they both peered at him with a mixture of fear and surprise. Kitty moved in for a closer inspection. She folded her arms across her chest and hugged herself. "I washed him myself. There was no dirt or blood or anything under those fingernails."

"No, it's fresh." He drew the tips of Otis's fingers across the back of his own hand. Faint traces of blood smeared his skin.

Kitty stepped back, gasping. "Holy Mother of God."

"I should have been here." Rebecca bit down on her knuckle.

"No." Jake forced her hand away from her mouth, and pulled her against his chest. "You would've been hurt, maybe killed. You did exactly what you should have done. Someone obviously wanted Otis dead, and nothing would've stopped him."

"What were you doing looking under his eyelids?" Kitty asked, her brows drawn together in suspicion.

"There are red dots around his eyes. It's called pete-chial—" He mentally chided himself for getting too literal. All that would get him was more questions. "The dots mean that his airway had been blocked, like if someone had been smothered or strangled, but in this case, the hanging—"

The blank looks stopped him. He was totally blowing it. More than ever he needed them to trust him. "I think it's better we don't tell anyone about my suspicion." He looked at Kitty waiting for her to object.

"I agree," she said, surprising him. "Not that I know what the hell to do about it, though."

"I do," Jake said, sighing.

Both women looked expectantly at him. Shit, he had some explaining to do.

_11_

JAKE PULLED THE SHEET over Otis's face as soon as the door closed behind Kitty. No sense exposing him to Rebecca any longer, and there was nothing more Jake could learn to help him find the killer. Not without a crime scene unit and a forensics lab, anyway.

They decided Kitty would go back to the saloon to break the news about Otis. Jake and Rebecca would follow soon, after the hoopla died down. Rebecca was still a wreck, no matter how much Jake had assured her that she wasn't to blame, and he wanted time alone with her to get her settled down.

Damn, he was being a fool. Doing exactly what he'd promised himself he wouldn't do. He was letting his feelings for Rebecca get in the way. The smart thing would be to go with Kitty and watch the reactions when she announced that Otis was dead. Most people were going to be surprised and saddened, but there would be relief, maybe even satisfaction on the face of the guilty party. Or more likely, guilty parties. Just a feeling Jake had.

To ease his conscience for not doing the right thing, he reasoned that Otis had marked his assailant and that was enough of a lead. Jake also needed time alone with

Rebecca. He wanted to know what she'd intended to do with that shard of glass he'd taken from her. He also needed to tell her more about his situation. The problem was, he still didn't know how much he should tell her about how he'd ended up in the 1800s. Would it be better for now to keep it simple and tell her he'd been sent from back East to investigate the corrupt Rangers?

"You're still shaking," he said, taking her cold hand in his. Even though Otis was covered, she stared at the form of his body beneath the sheet.

"It's cold."

"You're right. We need to get that fire going again." He urged her to the stove and made her participate with feeding in logs and stirring the dying coals.

She worked diligently, but he knew her mind was replaying the events of the last half hour. Hell, maybe it wasn't a good time to lay a bunch of crap on her that she wouldn't understand. Was he being selfish wanting her to get why he'd socialized with Wade? Her look of shocked disappointment at him sitting with Wade had been hard to chase from his mind. Still was.

"Was that the first dead body you've seen?" he asked, hoping that talking about the tragedy would help her detach.

She blinked at him, seeming surprised at first, and then grimly shook her head.

Right. Around here? She'd probably seen far more than any person should have to. "Do you know when the doctor is supposed to return?"

"No." She laughed humorlessly. "But it's too late for Doc Davis."

"He'll want to examine the body."

She stopped stirring the coals and looked quizzically at him. "Why? Mr. Otis is already dead."

Jake shrugged. "He might notice something that will help us find who did this."

She turned back to stare at the fire, undisguised anger in her eyes. "You know who did this."

This was his cue. "You do know why I was talking to Wade earlier, don't you?"

She tensed. "You want to work for him."

"It's not that I *want* to work for him. I might not have a choice."

Judging by the way she viciously stabbed at the logs, she wasn't convinced.

"Rebecca." He took the poker from her, set it down, and held both her hands, forcing her to face him. "There's something I have to tell you about me, but first, I need to know why you hid that piece of glass."

Her eyes widened. She stubbornly pressed her lips together, and then said softly, "For protection."

"I was afraid of that." He squeezed her hands. "You try to use something like that as a weapon, you'll only end up getting hurt. Maybe killed." He'd added the extra warning to frighten some sense into her, but she didn't seem fazed.

She didn't even blink. "I'd prefer a knife, but Kitty took that away from me."

"A knife?" Jake inwardly shuddered at the thought of her going up against one of those thugs with a knife. Didn't she understand what these men were capable of? No, sadly, she did. He could see the banked fear in her steady blue-green gaze, but she was also too brave for her own good. "Rebecca, you're no match for any of those men."

"They'll hurt me either way." Her voice was calm, resigned and she might as well have plunged that shard of glass right into his heart.

"No, they won't. Not while I'm alive." They stared into

each other's eyes for what seemed an eternity. "Can you trust me on that?"

She wanted to, he could see the yearning on her face. But there was doubt and fear, too, that primal struggle for survival because trusting anyone could make her weak and vulnerable. He hated it, but he understood that he hadn't yet earned her trust.

"Just for now, okay? Don't do anything to endanger yourself. Give me a chance to explain who I am, and what I need to do. If I'm still welcome, I'll come up to your room later, and we'll talk."

When she nodded, he slowly exhaled. Unfortunately, that wasn't even half the battle. If he told her the unvarnished truth, she'd be twice as fearful because she'd have him to worry about, as well. How could anyone believe he'd traveled through time? She'd think he was a total lunatic. Hell, he wasn't sure that he wasn't completely insane.

"Thank you," she whispered, lightly pressing her palms against his.

"What for?"

"For protecting me. For stopping that man from—" She briefly closed her eyes. "You've made trouble for yourself with Captain Wade. This could be very bad for you."

He reared his head back, and gave her a mock look of insult. "You don't think a big strong man like me can beat up Wade?"

She seemed startled at first, saw that he was teasing her, and then smiled.

"I like to see that," he told her, touching one corner of her mouth with the pad of his thumb. "You should smile more."

Apparently that had been the wrong thing to say. She pulled away from him, her lips thinning in a grim line.

"Rebecca."

She turned back to the fire. "You should go. I'll wait for Doc Davis."

"There's nothing more you can do here." Man, he did not want her sitting here with the dead man. She'd end up feeling morose and needlessly guilty again.

"I have my book to read."

A muted memory of her reading beside his bed when he'd wake up from his drugged sleep flashed in his mind. As curious as he was about Rebecca's book, he was more concerned with removing her from the death room. "Take it with you and read upstairs. It might not be safe for you here," he said, annoyed with the defiance that remained in her eyes. "The killer could return."

She blinked, and the rebelliousness faded, quickly to be replaced with a sad downturn of her lips. "I don't expect I'm much safer upstairs in the saloon."

"You will be with me there." He caught her hand and pressed a soft kiss to the back of it. "No one will enter your room. I swear it on my life."

Her wary eyes were focused on the spot where he'd kissed her hand, and then she lifted her gaze to his face, briefly touching on his lips. She moistened hers, and that was all the invitation he needed.

He lowered his head at the same time he lifted her chin, pleased to discover that she needed little prompting. She placed her hands on his chest and softened her lips when he coaxed her response. He asked permission with the tip of his tongue, and as soon as she parted her lips, swept into her sweet mouth.

Her fingers curled against his chest and when he wrapped his arms around her, she trembled slightly. Jake wished she'd participate more, mostly to reassure himself that she wanted this as much as he did. And then she sighed into his mouth, a soft contented sigh that made his heart catch.

He deepened the kiss, while exploring her narrow back, running his hands to the curve of her backside, then reeling himself in so he wouldn't spook her. She leaned into him, her small soft breasts pressing against his chest as she looped her arms around his neck. The shirt she'd altered for him was thin, as was the material of her dress and he easily felt her protruding nipples poking his chest. The sensation nearly drove him off the edge. His thickening cock twitched. Expecting her to shove him away, he braced himself.

Rebecca leaned more weight against him. She had to feel his arousal. No way she didn't know how turned on he was, yet she wasn't afraid of him. The small expression of trust pleased him, emphasized how much his next move mattered.

It took about everything he had, but he slowed down, gentled the kiss, and brought his hands to either side of her waist. She stiffened slightly, her arms going slack around his neck, before she pulled back to gaze at him with confused eyes.

He swooped back down to kiss the tip of her nose, and then nibble the corner of her mouth. With his teeth, he grazed her chin, her jawline, and finally the shell of her ear. When he flicked his tongue over her earlobe, she giggled. The perfect time to retreat. For her benefit. For him, no way in hell. In a minute he'd have to discreetly adjust his fly.

She blinked at him, and then quickly looked away as her face turned pink.

"I like kissing you," he whispered, touching her warm cheeks and then watching a strand of hair curl around his finger. "I want to kiss you some more, if you'll let me."

Her eyes widened slightly, in obvious surprise. Was she used to men who simply took what they wanted?

"But not here," he continued, not having expected a response. "Anyone could walk in."

Her startled gaze flickered toward the door, and she backed away. "Will you walk me back to the saloon?"

"Of course."

"You don't have to accompany me inside," she added quickly, picking up the brown wool wrap that she'd left on the stool. She drew it around her shoulders, trapping her hair.

Jake lifted the thick mass of curls free and let the silky locks sift through his fingers as they tumbled down her back. "Try and stop me."

She smiled shyly, a hint of hero worship in her doe eyes.

His heart constricted, and he suddenly didn't know what to think, or what to say. He quickly shoved his hands into his pockets. Tonight they would talk. She'd find out he was a Ranger. And God only knew what she'd think of him then.

WITH JAKE BESIDE HER, Rebecca walked through the doors of the saloon, each step she took more frightening than the last. The piano music seemed somber, not the lively tunes that often hurt her ears. The men weren't laughing loudly or joking with each other like they usually did this time of night. Shots of whiskey and glasses of beer crowded the tables, but only one group of men played cards near the stairs, and no one was cursing or fighting. Trixie and Ruby stood at the end of the bar with dour expressions, drinking together. Rebecca didn't think that was even allowed.

It was a strange night, though not unexpected, on account of Mr. Otis dying. She didn't know the rancher, and still she felt a wretchedness in the pit of her belly that wouldn't ease. If folks blamed her, she wouldn't fault them. But she was glad Jake and Kitty didn't, and that Jake had pointed out that there was nothing she could've done against a killer. That helped her shame some.

But there was more than a senseless death eating at her. She'd made a difficult decision a few minutes ago. Tonight she would tell Jake about her past. All of it, the slaying of her family, the five years she'd lived with the Comanche, she'd even tell him about her husband. The idea that she had to form the words and let them spill from her lips made her queasy again.

She was so confused about Jake at this point, she couldn't imagine how he would react to her admission. One minute he was cozying up to Captain Wade, and the next he was defending her at the cost of angering the captain. Jake Malone surely was the most unusual man she'd ever met, not that she'd met many. White men, anyway. But even Kitty agreed that Jake was different and unexpected, and heaven only knew how many men Kitty had known in her life. Poor Kitty. So kind and brave in many ways. How had she ended up in Diablo Flats? Why wouldn't she leave this horrible place?

Rebecca drew in a deep calming breath. She had her own problems to worry about. Even if she denied it aloud, she knew in her heart that she held onto a small hope that Jake would help her escape. Particularly when he kept befuddling her with his acts of nobility.

She spotted Kitty sitting at the bar drinking a glass of whiskey, and felt a measure of relief, until she noticed that Captain Wade sat beside her friend. Rebecca wanted to change direction, run for the safety of her room, but Jake walked beside her, his hand cupping her elbow as he steered them toward Kitty and the captain.

Almost as if her fear had willed him to seek her out, Captain Wade turned his head and watched them approach. He had the most unreadable face of any creature she'd ever met, even when he drank, though she'd never seen him drunk like some of the other Rangers. He reminded her of a snake that waited patiently and struck when a person least expected it.

"Any idea when Doc Davis will return?" Jake asked, leaning against the bar. He'd moved his hand from her elbow to the small of her back, which should have helped her feel protected, but only made her more nervous.

"Why?" Captain Wade snickered. "Sounds like Otis needs an undertaker, not a doctor."

"Jesus, Wade, show some respect," Kitty said, and then looked away and downed the rest of her whiskey when the captain glanced at her.

"Just stating a fact, darlin'." The captain's mouth curved slightly as he sipped from the foaming glass of beer.

"Too bad you never got him to talk first," Jake said, then shook his head at the offer of a whiskey.

One of the other Rangers sitting at the bar overheard and leaned toward them, his breath stinking with the odor of stale tobacco and cheap spirits. "Why? What would he have to say that we'd want to hear?"

Rebecca tried to step away, revulsion clogging her throat at the man's nearness. His face was so close to hers that it was hard not to be rude and openly cringe.

Jake kept his hand at her back and moved with her, putting some distance between her and the Ranger, whom he peered at as if the man were daft. "Gee, I don't know, maybe some information on the rustlers or who's behind the vigilante hangings."

The Ranger cursed violently, glaring at Jake with bloodshot eyes, his fingers tightening into a fist.

"Enough." Captain Wade put up a hand, gave Jake an impatient look, and then eyed the other Ranger. "Time you turned in, Vernon. Sleep off that whiskey. We got a long day tomorrow."

"What?" The look of shocked betrayal slid to anger on the Ranger's face and made Rebecca take another step back.

This time Jake didn't move with her. He stayed where he was between Captain Wade and the other Ranger. She understood that for him to have backed up would have shown weakness, but the knowledge didn't stop her insides from fluttering like leaves in the wind.

"And you need to shut up," Captain Wade said to Jake. "No good will come of us fighting amongst ourselves."

"You including him with us?" Vernon's face flushed an angry red and he couldn't seem to take his eyes off Jake.

"Look…" Jake's smile was slow and purposeful. "Vernon, right? You're pissed. I don't blame you. I shouldn't have shot off my mouth." He stuck out his hand. "No hard feelings?"

Vernon blinked at Jake's outstretched hand. He muttered a curse, picked his hat up off the bar and left.

The captain chuckled. "You're just full of surprises, ain't you, Malone?"

Jake shrugged. "I didn't mean to stir up the pot. But I'm not looking to make friends either. I was just saying…this Otis fella could've been useful."

Captain Wade grunted, his gaze going to Rebecca. "You, get out of here."

She stiffened, and as she picked up her skirt and turned, she met Jake's eyes. He gave her a small encouraging nod and glanced toward the stairs.

"You, too, Kitty. Get." The captain patted Kitty's fanny, and then laughed when Kitty glared at him.

She grabbed the half-full bottle of whiskey off the bar, and took it with her. Rebecca braced herself for the captain's reaction, but he said nothing as she and Kitty walked toward the back of the saloon.

"Stupid bastard," Kitty muttered.

Rebecca stared at her, never having seen Kitty in such a dark mood, or heard her say anything bad about the captain. "Are you going upstairs?"

"No, to the kitchen. I'm betting Cook could use a drink. He knew Otis from way back." They paused by the piano. "You go on upstairs. I doubt anyone will bother you tonight, and I'm betting Jake will be up shortly." Kitty started to go, and then whispered close to Rebecca's ear. "Tell him I haven't said a word about his suspicions about Otis being murdered, and I think he's right."

Rebecca watched her disappear down the short hall, and tried to shake the feeling of being watched herself. She glanced over her shoulder and scanned the room. No one seemed to be paying her any mind. Not even Jake. His attention was focused on what the captain was telling him. He looked particularly solemn as he listened, and she got a chill thinking about what she herself had to admit to him later.

For a moment she considered it could wait until morning, but that wouldn't be fair to him. If he kissed her again… She pressed her lips together, ashamed at how much she wanted another kiss, how much she wanted his hands on her. Her husband had been in the ground for only a year. A decent woman would still be in mourning.

Swallowing painfully, she gathered her skirt in one hand and reached for the railing with the other. Before her foot hit the first step, she sensed someone behind her. Out of the corner of her eye, she saw Corbin rushing from the hall. He yanked her backward, his fingers pinching into the tender flesh of her nape.

She let out a shriek that was smothered by the shrill notes of the piano. Corbin grabbed her arm and dragged her toward the narrow hall. She kicked at him, clawed at him, struggled to wrench her arm free, but his grip was too tight.

"Where's your boyfriend now?" he asked, his fetid breath slithering across her cheek. "Better not be giving it away, you ungrateful bitch."

She dared to look at him, and saw a wildness in his bleary eyes that terrified her. Three deep scratches slashed his cheek. Had she done that? Surely, he'd kill her. She opened her mouth to scream, but before she uttered a sound, a fist shot out and connected with Corbin's jaw.

He staggered backward, releasing her as he tried to regain his balance. Jake threw another punch that sent Corbin to the floor with a loud thud. He pushed up on one elbow, groaned when he couldn't get up and then fell back onto the hardwood floor.

He spat out some blood, and then fixed his evil glare on Jake. "Fine," Corbin said, "Go have your Indian whore."

_12_

THE URGE TO HIT Corbin herself, pulsed in Rebecca's veins.

She desperately wanted to silence him, to wipe the smug look off his face. But it was too late. He'd said the words that would doom her with Jake. How he must despise her for not having the courage to tell him herself. For allowing him to kiss a mouth that had already been claimed by an Indian.

Oh, God. The earth seemed to move beneath her feet, and her head felt so light, so wrong. It hurt where the Ranger had dug his filthy fingers into the side of her neck. God forgive her but she wished he were dead.

Jake touched her lower back. "Are you okay?"

She couldn't look at him. Why was he still being kind? Tears threatened, but she wouldn't cry. Not in front of Corbin. The pig. How she longed to spit in his face. If she did, maybe he would leap up and slit her throat, and it would all be over. The agony of the past weeks since the Rangers captured her would end.

"Rebecca?" Jake tried to catch her chin, but she jerked away from him.

Corbin laughed, the hacking sound echoing across the

suddenly silent saloon. "Look at that, he still wants you. Must be one of them Indian lovers. Ain't you the lucky whore?"

Jake moved so quickly she didn't realize what had happened until she saw his boot pressed into Corbin's chest. He started hacking again, his coughs so violent blood spewed from his mouth.

"I'm gonna tell you one more time, Corbin, to shut the hell up. After that, I won't be so nice." Jake eased his boot off the Ranger's chest. "Are we clear?"

"Jesus Christ, Malone." Captain Wade shoved aside two card players who'd stood to watch the fight. He frowned down at Corbin. "What the fuck is going on?"

Corbin turned his head to the side and spit out more blood.

The captain shook his head. It wasn't hard to read him now. His face was darker than thunderclouds as he eyed Jake. "You're starting to make me nervous, Malone, and I don't like feeling nervous. What the hell happened?"

Jake wearily rubbed the back of his neck, watching as the captain gave Corbin a hand up.

The Ranger staggered as he got to his feet, the fury in his eyes aimed at Jake. "This goddamn Indian lover—" Corbin cut himself off, clearly remembering that he was breaking the rules.

Another small piece of Rebecca's heart broke off and shattered. What did it matter what Corbin said now? Enough of the men heard what he'd said earlier. By now most of them knew she'd been bedded by an Indian. By the end of the night, they would all know. But she only cared that one did, and Jake was showing no reaction, other than the hatred that burned in his eyes for Corbin.

He must have seen it, too. The Ranger wiped his mouth with the back of his sleeve, at the same time, circling around

Jake and the captain, his angry gaze darting between the two men. One of the card players picked his hat up off the floor and passed it to him. He snatched it with a muttered curse, and left the saloon.

Captain Wade poked a finger in Jake's face. "I don't need trouble."

Jake's gaze narrowed on the captain's finger, and then he slowly moved it away. "What did you expect?" he asked in a low controlled voice. "Did you think your men were going to welcome me with open arms?"

The captain hooked his thumbs in his gun belt, his steely gaze fixed on Jake.

"They don't know me," Jake continued. "They don't like me and they don't trust me. There are gonna be scrapes. It'll be up to me to keep my cool."

Captain Wade barked out a harsh laugh. "By laying them out on the floor?"

Unexpectedly, one side of Jake's mouth lifted. "Yeah, well, shit happens."

Even more unexpected, Captain Wade looked as if he wanted to smile. But he didn't. His jaw jutting out, he studied Jake for a moment. "You let pussy get in the way of business, that makes you a goddamn fool. I don't need fools working for me."

"I hear you."

Captain Wade slid a brief look at Rebecca where she'd shrunk back into the corner. "Get out of my sight," he told Jake. "Now." The Ranger turned toward the back, and yelled for Kitty.

With his eyes and chin, Jake motioned for Rebecca to ascend the stairs. She quickly obeyed, horribly afraid her wobbly legs wouldn't carry her the entire way to her room. But Jake was right behind her, guiding her with his hand, ignoring the stares that followed them. When they got to her door, she turned to thank him for the escort, loath to meet the disappointment she was sure to find in his eyes. But he startled her by opening the door, urging her inside and following her.

She quickly lit the lantern, the click of the door closing behind him stealing her breath. Didn't he understand that he could no longer be with her? Even if nothing happened, the closed door would surely feed rumors. The men downstairs would talk…they'd shun him for knowingly taking an Indian whore…

"Are you all right?" He gently took her by the shoulders, his anxious gaze roaming her face. This was no longer the Jake who'd stood up to Captain Wade.

"Yes," she whispered, scarcely able to find her voice. "You have to go."

"Why?" With his fingers, he gently probed the tender skin Corbin had dug into. "You're going to bruise. I should've killed the bastard," he murmured, so low, she almost didn't hear.

"Jake?"

He put his arms around her and held her against his chest. "You're safe now. I promise."

"Don't you understand?" She didn't, not what was happening now. Had he been so angry that he hadn't heard what Corbin said? It didn't matter. Everyone else knew.

"I'm so sorry. That was my fault." He leaned back to look at her. "I thought you'd be safe to go as far as the stairs with Kitty. Please forgive me, Rebecca."

"Oh, Jake, I'm fine." She felt the tears fill her eyes, and she quickly laid her cheek against his chest so he wouldn't see her crying. He'd think she was hurt when she wasn't. She wasn't sure what she felt right now, humbled, grateful, frightened. Her insides were a jumbled mess like a ball of yarn that had been strewn across the room by a mischievous cat and tangled so badly she couldn't unravel it.

He lapsed into silence for several nerve-racking moments. "I'm also sorry for what happened to you," he said, his voice strained.

She froze, blinking hard, willing the tears to stop before he tried to look at her. "It'll be only a small bruise," she said, knowing in her heart that wasn't what he meant.

"Not that. What happened to you before." His tone was gentle, not in the least condemning. "Tell me about it."

She tensed, and pulled away, but he caught her hand. That's when he saw she'd been crying. He used his thumb to wipe the moisture from her cheeks, his expression so grim she wanted to start crying all over again.

"I was going to tell you tonight," she said brokenly. "You deserved to know."

"Deserve?" He frowned. "I don't know about that, but I'll listen to anything you *want* to tell me. Anything that isn't too painful for you to relive." He tugged at her hand and drew her to the bed, helping her to sit at the edge as if she were a fragile porcelain doll.

She had no choice. That he was still willing to touch her, his face full of tenderness and concern, made her so weak she'd crumble if she didn't sit.

He pushed his fingers through her hair, combing through the tangles, and then arranged the long messy curls over her shoulder, away from her face. She almost wished he hadn't, because now she felt too exposed. But he gave her an encouraging smile, and all her defenses seemed to melt.

"Talk to me," he said in a low voice, husky with emotion.

She moistened her dry lips, summoning her courage and preparing herself. Once he heard the words from her own mouth, he might not be so understanding. "It happened five years ago," she said slowly, searching his face for loathing, now that he knew it hadn't been for a week or a month or even a year since she'd been removed from white society.

He said nothing, simply waited patiently, his eyes now neutral, while he continued stroking the back of her hand.

"My parents and brother and I were traveling from Fort Belknap." She stopped, unprepared for the stab of a painful memory from the night they were attacked. The screams, the flames, the smell of fear and desperation...the shrill cries of the warriors as they threw their heads back in victory.

Jake frowned. "On your own?"

"We'd started out with a wagon train from the Kansas railyard, but Father said it would be faster if we—" She stared down at her lap, knowing now, years later, that the tragedy could have been avoided if not for her father's stubbornness. But to put a voice to the knowledge would make her a traitor to his memory. "We were warned it could be bad."

He nodded without judgment. "How old were you?"

She sighed. "We were celebrating my nineteenth birthday that night."

"Ah, Rebecca." He leaned over and pressed his forehead against hers. "I'm sorry."

"My brother had turned thirteen two days before," she whispered. "Father had given Seth our grandfather's rifle as a birthday present. Mother was worried about him learning how to shoot." Her voice cracked as the irony hit her.

Jake drew back, his eyes concerned. "You don't have to talk about it."

She shrugged helplessly. "I don't remember very much. Not about that night. It all happened so fast. There were a dozen Comanche or more. Before coming West, we'd lived in Philadelphia. Father was a lawyer. He seldom used a gun. He was no match for—" She covered her face, unable to go on.

"Shh, it's all right." He gathered her in his arms and held her tight. "It's all right."

"No, you don't understand." She broke free, her face feeling hot and flushed. "I lived with them, ate with them, slept with them. I had no choice." That wasn't true. She'd had many chances to kill herself, but she'd been a coward.

"Of course you had no choice. You survived. That's all that matters."

She sadly shook her head and lowered her gaze. "A decent woman would not have endured such shame."

He brought her chin back up, and looking genuinely puzzled, said, "What shame? You were a captive."

"I heard the women from the wagon train whisper while they washed the supper dishes. They all vowed to never be taken alive by Indians. They said the decent thing for a woman to do was to…release herself."

"I don't pretend to understand your customs," he said slowly, distracting her for a second because it was such an odd thing for him to say. "But that's plain wrong."

"No, I heard them, but I was too afraid. I had many chances, but I—"

"Listen to me." He wouldn't let her hide, but framed her face with his hands and looked her square in the eyes. "Unless you're threatened with death, taking a life, even your own, is never the right thing to do. You did exactly what you were supposed to do. You stayed alive."

"But—"

He lightly drew his thumb across her lower lip, cutting her off. "Believe me, I can't say I wouldn't put a bullet between any man's eyes for hurting you. But that wouldn't be justice, it would be vengeance, and I'd like to think I'm better than that." He smiled faintly. "Don't get me wrong. I've done things in my life I regret, things that I never dreamed I would consciously do. No one knows how they'll react until they're actually in a situation. I bet not one of those women you heard talking would actually take her own life. And certainly not a God-fearing woman."

Oh, how she wanted to believe him. She'd told herself the same thing many times, but it hadn't helped. "They weren't all bad," she said slowly, studying his reaction, preparing herself for his revulsion. "The Comanche who I lived with."

Relief relaxed his jaw, softened his mouth, and made her want to weep. "I'm glad," he said, placing a light kiss on her cheek. "That's something." He had more questions. She could see them smoldering in the dark blue depths of his eyes.

But he didn't ask. Instead he moved his hands from her face to comb back her hair, and then brushed his lips to hers, a gentle featherlike touch that told her more than his words. He didn't blame her. The knowledge gave her courage.

"The braves who attacked our camp knew there was a company of soldiers from Fort Belknap patrolling the area so they didn't linger. They took our horses and milk cow and the only three rifles Father owned, a few of Mother's trinkets and then threw me over the back of a horse. I was lucky in that we rode quickly…" She hoped he caught her meaning, and added, "With no stops until we got to their village."

His eyebrows went up slightly, and then he nodded. She hoped he understood that she hadn't been brutalized, at least not in the way most white people assumed, but with Jake it was difficult to tell. He'd shown none of the reactions of loathing and horror she'd suffered from the Rangers. His sympathy for her was earnest and heartwarming.

"Once we arrived, Running Bear, one of the war chief's sons immediately claimed me. I was terrified, bloodied and badly bruised. His mother took pity on me and kept me with her until I healed. I honestly don't remember much of that, only what I was told later."

"I have to admit, I know only a little about the history of the Comanche people," Jake said. "I have a friend who's half Comanche but—" He smiled suddenly. "That explanation is for later."

She couldn't wait for later. A white man who had a Comanche friend? Not unheard of, she supposed, but rare. Even when her family had stopped at the Fort, she'd heard nothing but unkind remarks about the Indians. "Your friend is a scout?"

"No." Jake drew out the word. "He works with me sometimes but it's hard to explain."

"What is his name?"

"Tom."

Rebecca blinked. "Yes?"

"Tom Parker."

"He has no other name?" She didn't understand. The Comanche were fiercely proud people. A brave would not take a white man's name easily, even if he was a half-breed.

Jake shifted, stretching out his back, and then held his side and winced.

"You hurt yourself again."

"I'm just stiff. Tell me more about Running Bear."

Rebecca sighed. "He was not so hateful of the white man as were his brothers. Like his father, he wanted peace."

"Did he treat you well?"

She nodded, knowing the truth of what he asked. "He made me his wife."

"Ah." Jake didn't look pleased. He moved the hand he'd placed on hers and rubbed his jaw. But she knew there was no itch he needed to satisfy. He no longer wished to touch an Indian bride. "How did you end up here?"

"The men had gone hunting and there were only a few of us working in the village when the Rangers came." Another memory she wanted banished from her mind. "Three older boys had stayed behind to protect the women and children. They were killed, but everyone else scattered into the woods." Rebecca shrugged. "One of the Rangers saw my hair and they chased me into the trees while the other women got away."

Abrupt anger darkened Jake's features. "Were they shooting at the women and children?"

She said nothing. As much as she wanted the Rangers to pay for their cruelty, she didn't want Jake involved. He was one man. They were many.

"Bastards," he muttered, exhaling sharply. He touched her hand again, and then quickly retreated, folding his hands together and letting them dangle between his knees. "So I guess your husband must be looking for you."

"Running Bear is dead."

His head drew back. "When?"

"Over a year now."

"I'm sorry." He didn't look sorry. Oddly, he looked almost pleased. "I am. I'm sorry for your loss, but I'm—Oh, crap. I'm an ass." He abruptly stood and paced to the small window over the dresser.

Rebecca hesitated, but then couldn't sit still another second. Following him to the window, she dared to lay a hand on his arm, ready to pull back if he showed signs of anger. "I don't understand."

"You're mourning the loss of your husband, and God help me, I'm sitting here glad that you're single—that you're free. That I can kiss you and touch you and not feel guilty as hell."

Relief spilled through her. "I too am sorry he's dead. He didn't deserve to die at the hands of the filthy Comanchero. But Running Bear had not been a husband to me for two years before he was killed."

Jake's eyes narrowed as he considered what she was trying to tell him. "I hate to speak ill of the dead, but that man was a fool," he said quietly. "You're so beautiful. How could he stay away?"

"He had two other wives." Rebecca cleared her throat. Whatever pride she had once possessed was gone. Left in the ashes of her family's camp all those years ago. "They bore him children."

"So he abandoned you?"

Would Jake never stop surprising her? She had all but admitted that she was barren, but still he hadn't recoiled from her. "No, I was still part of his family. His mother and I grew very close. She taught me many things. I owe Bird Song my life."

"Then I owe her, as well." He lowered his head and kissed one side of her mouth, and then trailed his lips to the bruised spot where Corbin had dug his hard fingers into her flesh.

Rebecca's eyes drifted closed, hoping with all her heart that this was real and not a dream. No man had ever treated her so tenderly. Certainly not her husband. She didn't know this was possible. Many times in the past five years she'd given up her belief in God. But now she knew He did exist. He'd sent her Jake.

13

JAKE TRACED the delicate shell of her ear and then flicked the lobe with his tongue. He couldn't remember ever feeling this humbled and irrational about a woman. Touching her, hearing her voice, merely inhaling her earthy feminine scent stirred every protective instinct in his being. The whole thing was crazy and dangerous because his reaction to her was throwing him off his game. If he weren't more careful in the future, he'd end up getting them both killed.

Thinking about the incident with Corbin, Jake cursed his own stupidity. Bad enough he'd been lax in monitoring Rebecca's movements until he knew she was safely in her room, but then he'd unthinkingly plowed after the Ranger without regard for the careful trap he'd been laying for the captain. If the man couldn't bring himself to trust Jake, there'd be no helping anyone.

He realized how turned on he was getting, and promptly lifted his head. How could he be such an ass? She'd just explained about losing her husband. It didn't matter that the man had been too foolish to treat her like a proper wife. He had been a part of Rebecca's life. To some degree, he'd kept her safe. For that, Jake owed him his respect and gratitude.

"I'm sorry, Rebecca," he said, aware that he'd said those words more in the past couple of days than he had in his whole life. Cupping her shoulders, he set her back. "I didn't mean to get carried away."

Her eyes were huge and shining, her lips coated with a sheen of moisture. "Don't be sorry," she said shyly, and tentatively put a palm against his chest. "Why aren't you like the others?"

Now that he knew she wasn't innocent, that she'd been with a man, it still didn't add up for him. She had to know how worked up he'd been getting, how the way she was moving closer to him would only make him want her more. "The other Rangers?"

She blinked. "The other white men. Even Kitty and Lola said no white man would touch me if they knew I'd been bedded by an Indian. Captain Wade and the Rangers only kept the secret so they could use me when the railroad men came to town."

The thought of how she'd been treated by the so-called lawmen sent a shaft of white-hot fury through him. The kind of blinding anger that he'd better restrain and quick. He breathed in deeply, reminded himself of what was at stake, and his sense of control slowly returned. This was the perfect time to tell her about himself, to explain that in the future, the ignorance against Indians no longer existed. He winced inwardly, knowing that wasn't entirely true, but close enough for her frame of reference.

"You don't have to worry about the railroad men, or any other man that you don't choose to invite into your room. Do you understand?" Although he didn't say so, he included himself. She needed comfort and an empathetic

ear, not his desire to strip her naked and kiss every inch
of her body.

She nodded, though she didn't look convinced, and then
a tiny smile tugged at the corners of her lips. "You shouldn't
have taken away my broken glass."

He started to smile back, but then the implication of
what she'd said struck him. "Rebecca, I respect that you're
willing to defend yourself, but the truth is, if you were to
fight a man, you'd probably be the one to get hurt."

She sighed. "That's what Kitty said when she took away
my knife."

He shook his head. She'd be better off with a gun. At
least then she'd have a chance. "If a man is close enough
for you to use a knife or shard of glass, he'll be able to
overpower you. Are you getting that?"

She frowned at his frustrated tone, her chin going up,
her hand falling away from his chest.

He hadn't meant to sound so sharp. "Maybe if I could
somehow get you a gun..."

Her eyebrows shot up. "I don't know how to use a gun.
But I'm very good with a knife."

Jake flashed back on the time she'd helped him to sit
up after he'd come to. He remembered then thinking how
deceptively strong she was for such a petite woman. Now
he understood. Living in an Indian village had required
physical endurance and skills most women would never
dream of. Rebecca undoubtedly was excellent with a knife,
but he still didn't like the idea of her carrying one.

"Tell you what," he said, stepping back as far as he could
without knocking over the basin and stool behind him. "I'm
going to show you a few moves that will stop a man long
enough for you to get away from him."

"A knife will do that."

He groaned. "Enough with the knife. I mean it." He

immediately regretted the words and the tone. She gave him a resentful glare, which he deserved. Men had been running her life for too long. She didn't need hearing that kind of crap from him. He closed the distance between them once again and cupped his hand around her slender nape. "If I sound stern or harsh it's because I'm scared for you. I don't want anything to happen to you."

She tilted her head slightly, her curious blue-green eyes fixed on his face. "Why?"

"That's a funny question." Tensing, Jake drew back his hand. "Because I worry about you." He cleared his throat. "Kitty worries about you."

Rebecca showed no reaction, not even disappointment over his cowardice. Why couldn't he have simply admitted that he cared for her? He did. Nothing serious. She was a human being, a mistreated woman, and he'd sworn to uphold the law.

And then the reason for her lack of reaction struck him, hard, right in the gut. She didn't expect anyone to care about her. Her husband's mother had been kind, but that didn't mean Rebecca wasn't used to being on her own and depending on herself for survival.

"Look," he said. "I care about you, that's why." He shoved his hand through his hair, frustrated. He couldn't even get that out right.

Rebecca smiled, almost as if she understood the turmoil roiling inside him. Glad someone did.

"You ready for your lesson?" Stepping back again, he rolled his shoulders, trying to loosen up the tension that had settled at the base of his neck and between his shoulder blades.

She nodded, her hands fisting at her sides.

"There are three ways you can either stop or slow down a man who attacks you. Depending on your position if you're attacked, you should go for the eyes, the throat or the groin area. These are all vulnerable areas that with a well-placed kick or flat-handed—"

Her brows furrowed, she regarded him as if he were speaking a different language.

What a dumb ass. He'd shifted gears, gone into Jake Malone, Texas Ranger, the third Saturday of every month, women's self-defense instructor. He'd taken on the volunteer assignment for a year before going undercover. It seemed like a decade ago. In reality, his current reality, it hadn't even happened yet. Hell, he still wasn't sure he wasn't totally insane. But gazing at Rebecca, he sincerely hoped not. He needed her to be real. Flesh and blood. This woman who stirred all kinds of crazy emotions inside of him.

He had to finally tell her the truth about himself. Right after the lesson.

"I think it's best that I show you, okay?" He waited for her hesitant nod, and then demonstrated the precursor for the open-hand technique. "Hold your hand like this."

Her nose wrinkled in concentration, she mimicked his stance, and made him want to laugh. He didn't dare.

"This is how you would knock the air out of him." He delivered a mock blow to her throat. "Hit him hard enough and he won't be able to catch his breath. He'll double over, trying to breathe, and you run."

She nodded uncertainly.

When he was done explaining, they'd practice and she'd feel more confident. "The eyes are another good place to strike." He made a V with his middle and forefinger. "Poke him in both eyes just like this," he said demonstrating on himself. "He'll panic and not be able to see. If your attacker is drunk, you've got a good shot using either one of these tactics. If he's not, and too tall, being as short as you are might be a problem. But you have other options."

She waited expectantly, while getting comfortable with forming her hand in a karate chop. She was a determined student, he'd give her that. Her serious attention sure made him feel more comfortable that she could defend herself.

"Now, what I'm about to explain is your best bet at disabling a man long enough so that you can get away before he recovers. You'll use your knee, by bringing your leg up like this and hitting him in the groin."

Rebecca stared blankly at him. Did she not understand the word *groin,* he wondered, or was she embarrassed?

He cupped a hand over his fly, drawing her gaze. "This is where you're aiming. It's a very sensitive area and—"

Her mouth quivered, and she quickly pressed her lips together. But not before he got that she was trying not to laugh.

He couldn't help but chuckle. "Yes? What's so funny?"

Her cheeks turned pink, but she still looked as if she were on the verge of laughing. "Nothing."

"I figure you know what's down here," he said, cupping himself more soundly, while torturing himself at the same time.

"Yes," she said, and laughed in earnest.

"Well, fine." He moved his hand. "I hope this is a joke and not something I have to take personally."

She dabbed at her eyes. "Oh, it was long ago, three years maybe…one of the young braves, his name is Blue Sky." She paused, her cheeks turning a deeper shade of rose.

"You have to tell me now."

She visibly swallowed. "Blue Sky was showing off, trying to get Moon Dance to notice him when he slid from a tree. He didn't see the stump. After that the squaws called him Blue Balls." She started to laugh again and quickly covered her mouth.

"Ouch." Jake winced in sympathy for the poor bastard. "You laugh, but let me tell you, that's about as painful as it gets for a man."

She touched her throat. "I know," she said, sobering. "That was very rude of me to laugh."

He smiled. "I like hearing you laugh." He winked. "As long as it's not at me."

Her expression turned wistful. "I used to laugh all the time. Twice I got in trouble at school for laughing, but I was a very good student so Father never took a switch to me."

Man, he had so many questions for her. But he'd feel more relaxed once he was convinced she could take care of herself when he wasn't around. "Speaking of being a good student, let's get back to your lesson."

She squared her shoulders, and spread her feet apart as he'd demonstrated earlier, looking like a warrior preparing for battle. Most of her long blond hair fell down her back, but a thick lock curled over one breast, calling attention to a protruding nipple that prodded the thin fabric of her dress. The way she looked right now would disarm any man, catch him off guard long enough for her to do some damage. Hell, she was doing a number on him, all right.

"Okay, back to kneeing the groin," he said, looking away from her breasts. "Don't be shy about making his b—this area here—the target." He passed a hand over his fly, discomfited by her unwavering stare.

It took him a second to realize he'd hardened, and that the longer she stared, the more his cock thickened.

Damn. That hadn't gone as planned.

He shifted, and she finally blinked. What now? Did he

apologize? Pretend nothing happened? Except if he didn't adjust his jeans soon, she'd be calling him Blue Balls II.

She cautiously lifted her gaze to his, and he couldn't tell if she were embarrassed, naive or getting heated herself. No, not naive. He didn't think embarrassed either, which left…

Okay, so maybe his time traveling tale could wait.

"Rebecca?"

She took a couple of steps toward him, lifting her face and parting her lips. Longing was stamped on her delicate features, a longing that closely mirrored his own.

If he did this, if he made love to her like he so desperately wanted to, could he move forward objectively? So much was at stake, so much that depended on him keeping a clear head and not getting them both killed. Getting him back to his own time.

She gingerly placed her hands on his chest. "I don't want to hurt you."

"I almost forgot about my ribs."

With a featherlike touch, she traced his lower lip. "The blisters are gone."

"I noticed that when I was shaving." He probed the corner of his mouth where the worst offender was now a faint scar which he knew would soon disappear. He smiled, and then brushed his lips across hers. "It doesn't hurt at all."

She moved her hand to the healing gash at the side of his head. "And here? Is it better?"

"Much." He wasn't lying. Until now it hadn't occurred to him that he'd not had a single headache since yesterday. "Maybe you should check my side."

"I should," she agreed, her eyes warm and knowing as she moved back and unsnapped his shirt.

Impatient, he helped her and then shrugged out of the scratchy flannel. The way she ogled his chest did his male ego good. No matter what mission he'd been assigned, even when working undercover, he'd always made time for exercise. He told himself that keeping physically fit was necessary for the job, but he knew damn well part of it was vanity. Right now, his diligence was paying off big-time.

Rebecca smoothed her palms over his pecs, immediately bringing his nipples to attention. She touched them, too, lightly with the tip of her finger, with a fascination that didn't make sense. She had to have seen more than her share of naked male chests.

"You have a lot of muscle," she said, briefly gazing up at him, and then following the course of her hands as they moved down to his ridged belly. "Everywhere."

"I work at it."

Her brows drew together in a puzzled frown, but she didn't ask any more questions, just returned to exploring him with her hands and eyes, everywhere but the intended spot.

"How do my ribs look?" he asked, belatedly hoping his teasing didn't scare her away.

Her lips twitched, and she focused her attention on his side. "The bruises will last awhile."

"Yep."

With a cheeky glint in her eyes, she met his gaze. "Does it hurt anywhere else?"

"Over here a little bit." He rubbed the side of his upper thigh, thankful he'd rebounded. She'd caught him off guard with her return volley. "Better have a look."

"Yes." She moistened her lips, and then showed some hesitation as she moved her hands to the waistband of his jeans.

"Here." He quickly unsnapped and unzipped, not wanting to lose their momentum.

Her fascinated gaze watched as he drew his jeans down his hips. He was forced to stop.

His boots. Damn.

It hurt to bend over so he sat at the edge of the bed. It still hurt like hell.

Rebecca dropped to the floor and knelt before him. She tugged up each hem until she got to the tops of his boots and then pulled off one, and then the other. Her dress had slid off her shoulder as it often did. He understood now why her clothes all seemed too big for her. They were borrowed, probably from Trixie, who was closest to Rebecca's size.

Her gaping neckline provided a hell of a view from where he sat, and certainly didn't help his aroused condition. She had small perfect breasts, crowned by dusky rose nipples that stood out like two plump cherries.

She glanced up suddenly, and there was no way he could deny he'd been blatantly looking down her dress. Blinking, she sat back on her heels and stared uncertainly at him.

"You're beautiful, Rebecca," was all he was inspired to say.

Her chest rose and fell with a deep shuddering breath. "I'm—" She shook her head. "I have scars," she whispered.

His memory flicked to the one he'd seen on her wrist the day she'd dressed his wounds. "Let me see them."

She shrunk back, folding her arms across her chest. "Can we put out the lantern?"

"Later. If you still want to." He caught her hand and drew her closer, so that she was back up on her knees. "But I have a couple of scars I want to show you first."

Her brows drew together in suspicion, but her gaze dutifully followed his hands as he gingerly pushed the bulky denim down to his thighs. She must've noticed the effort it took him, what with his ribs starting to ache, and she finished the job for him.

She shoved the jeans aside, and then stared at his dark brown boxers. Thank God he'd done laundry last week or they could've been the ones with pink hearts he'd been given as a joke last Valentine's Day.

Tentatively she fingered the finely spun fabric, and then looked up at him in awe. "What is this?"

"Not silk, but something like it," he said, realizing that she'd never seen anything like boxers before. That didn't appease him much. Hell, he had a hard-on the size of Oklahoma, and she was more interested in the material? Granted, the way he was sitting, most of his arousal was disguised. But still. "This is what I wanted to show you." He pulled the elastic waist down enough to expose the thick long scar across his lower hip.

Her eyes widened. "How did that happen?"

"Youth and arrogance. Found out the hard way that being able to climb on the back of a bull doesn't make you a bullrider."

He slipped the boxers all the way down, and tossed them on the floor. His thick hard cock sprung up, and he was immensely satisfied to hear her startled gasp. "This one here is from a bullet," he continued, pointing to the round scar located on his upper thigh. "I'd love to tell you I earned it in the line of duty but the sorry truth is, when I was seventeen, a friend and I were—"

She wasn't listening, only staring openmouthed at his fully aroused cock. After a moment, she pulled herself out of her preoccupation and looked up at him, her expression dazed.

Jake grinned. "That's my point, sweetheart," he said,

slipping the dress from her other shoulder, and sliding it down to bare both her sweet round breasts. "I won't be paying any attention to your scars either."

14

REBECCA TRIED NOT TO SHAKE as Jake lowered his head and kissed the tops of her breasts. With her neckline and sleeves pulled down, her arms trapped against her body, so much of herself bared, she would have panicked facing any other man. But not Jake. Never Jake. He was strong yet gentle, tough yet kind, handsome and smart, too. He was like no other man she'd ever known.

"I want to take this dress off you," he whispered, shoving back her hair so that he could kiss the side of her neck, using his lips, his tongue and taking soft nips with his teeth.

She'd never been kissed there before, not like that, and she very much liked it. Closing her eyes, her heart beating faster, her breath quickening, she let her head fall back and savored the different sensations.

"Okay, Rebecca?"

She couldn't recall the question, but she nodded her agreement. How could she refuse anything Jake asked of her?

"Come here."

She opened her eyes, and he was smiling at her, his face

still smooth from his shave, a thick lock of dark wavy hair falling across his forehead.

He leaned over and took her by the elbows. "Come sit here with me."

After untangling her skirt from her legs, she let him help her to her feet. But he stopped her from sitting, instead, looping his arms around her middle and bringing her breasts to his mouth. She watched as he touched the tip of his tongue to her nipple, circling it and then drawing the tight bud into his mouth, and suckling her like a hungry child.

She felt her body grow warm all the way down to her toes, and she clutched his shoulders. His hot moist mouth on her skin made crazy things go on in her head, made her grow wet between her thighs. It took her a minute to notice that he was unfastening the row of tiny buttons down the front of Trixie's dress.

Rebecca tensed. Bird Song had treated the scars on her back and arms with salve, and they weren't so harsh as they had been five years ago, but would Jake still think her beautiful once he laid eyes on them? Then she thought about Jake's scars and what he'd said about not noticing them, and she almost burst out laughing.

"These buttons are a challenge for my big clumsy fingers," he said, frustration in his face as he looked up at her. "Help me."

She heard a man's voice just outside the door, and abruptly turned her head, worried someone was about to barge in. Then she heard Lola's throaty laughter, and then their voices fading toward her room at the end of the balcony.

"We didn't lock the door." Jake kissed her briefly and then got up to make sure the door was bolted.

Even his back and buttocks were nicely muscled, and she

found herself plucking feverishly at the buttons securing her cuffs. By the time he'd returned to help her, she secretly acknowledged he was right. She hadn't noticed either of his scars. Her problem was trying not to stare at his manhood, so long and thick, the crown already glistening with moisture.

He was right about his fingers, too. They were big and clumsy and the more he fumbled with the tiny buttons, the harder it was for her not to laugh.

"I have never seen so damn many buttons on one piece of clothing," he grumbled. "Good grief. Just when I think I've gotten to the last one…"

"Yes, I much prefer a deerskin dress." The words were out of her mouth before she could call them back. Sorry she'd served him a reminder, she bit down hard on her lip, waiting for his reaction. He'd been kind so far, but he wouldn't want her past rubbed in his face.

Jake smiled. "I'd kind of like to see you in one of those."

"Truly?" A tight little lump rose in her throat.

"Sure." He teased her nipple with his thumb and forefinger, and she arched her back, warming with his touch. "Plus, with a deerskin dress, I could get you naked quicker." He put his mouth where his fingers had been, and rolled his tongue over the tight nub.

She felt the last button loosen, unaware of how he'd accomplished the feat. The dress slipped down to her hips, and then he slid it past her thighs to the floor, until all she wore was hastily sewn beige muslin pantalets. He loosened the drawstring waist, and then they too were gone.

Jake leaned back to look at her, his eyes hooded, his nostrils flaring slightly. Then his gaze drew to her right wrist where the scar from the tough buffalo hide bindings hadn't faded as well as on her other wrist. He picked up her hand and gently pressed a kiss to the ruined flesh. "I'm sorry you suffered," he murmured against her skin. "I wish I could take it all away, erase the horror."

"The braves tied me to the horse when they first caught me. I made it worse by struggling," she said, self-consciously touching her wrist, refusing to ruin this moment by thinking about that horrible night.

He kissed the spot again, and then picked up her other wrist and kissed that scar, as well. "I feel so damn helpless. And angry. And—"

"No," she whispered, pulling her hand out of his grasp and placing a finger to his lips. "No. It's done."

His eyes darkened to the color of midnight. "You're right."

He made sure the bed was clear, the lumps smoothed away and then he laid her back with such gentleness she shivered in his arms. He asked if she were cold, and only then did she notice the chill in the air, but she shook her head because with his warm body pressed to hers she felt nothing but the strong beat of his heart against her breast, and the heat of his arousal heavy on her belly.

He moved to lie beside her, cupping her breast, laved it gently and then flattened his palm over her belly. She stayed still, enjoying his touch, waiting for him to move his hand lower, but mostly she wanted very much to touch him. Would he object? Would he welcome her advance?

"You're tense," he whispered. "Am I hurting you?"

"No, I just—" She couldn't say it.

The pressure of his hand eased. "Tell me, Rebecca."

"I want to touch you, too," she said softly, feeling the heat of embarrassment surge up her chest and into her face.

"Ah, good." He rolled onto his back. "I'm all yours. Any way you want."

She heard the amusement in his voice and tried to ignore it. The only man she'd ever been with was her husband, and he'd always been quick to get the job finished. At first, she'd been grateful. Later, as acceptance grew, so had her curiosity.

Cautiously she splayed her fingers across Jake's chest, and stared down at his hard shaft. She wanted to touch him there, find out if it was as hard as it looked. Swallowing, she slid a peek at his face, and found him watching her. "Don't do that."

One side of his mouth went up. "What?"

"I can't do anything if you watch."

"Okay, I won't." His shoulders came off the mattress, and he latched his lips onto her nipple.

She jerked in surprise, saw his smile, and her heart fluttered. He was a most baffling man. She stared down again at his manhood, moist and pulsing. With her finger, she lightly touched the tip. It leaped at her, and she quickly withdrew her hand.

Jake moaned. "Don't stop there."

She smiled, and traced a blue vein down to the base. His manhood again leaped at her touch. This time she didn't pull away. She wrapped her fingers around him, amazed at the amount of heat coming from his shaft. His mouth moved from her breast, and he lay back down, his eyes closed. She tentatively slid her hand up and then back down, something she had seen Sleeping Fox do to himself by the river one summer day.

When Jake moved his hips to match the rhythm of her hand, she knew she was doing it right. But then she might have squeezed too hard because he abruptly stilled her hand.

She swallowed back a lump of fear. "Did I hurt you?"

"No." He brought her hand to his lips and kissed the

back. "No way." He gave a shaky laugh and raised himself on one elbow.

She didn't believe that she hadn't hurt him because she saw pain skip across his face as he shifted. Sweat had popped out on his forehead. How could she have been so rough and careless?

His eyebrows drew together in a stern frown. "You didn't hurt me. I swear. I did it to myself just now when I tried to get up. But it's no big deal."

Rebecca moistened her lips. He had the strangest way of speaking sometimes. She saw her dress on the floor and reached for it. "You're still healing. We shouldn't have tried to—"

"No, you don't." He grabbed the dress from her, and tossed it toward the wall. Before she knew what had happened, he slid his hand between her thighs, his fingers skimming the nest of curls there. "It just means that I might be more comfortable with you on top."

She fell back on the mattress, trying to puzzle out what he was saying, when all she could do was focus on where his hand was headed. "I don't understand."

His fingers dove deeper, breaching the lips that hid her secret woman's place. Gasping, she brought her knees up and clenched her muscles, but that only made him groan as he pushed further, entering the narrow passage with his fingers.

"Rebecca. You're so wet."

She wanted to cover her ears. Why would he want to embarrass her so? But the look on his face told her he wasn't trying to do any such thing. She'd somehow pleased him. Startled, she eased her legs apart, just a little, so that her thighs weren't clamped so tightly over his hand. He withdrew a bit, and then plunged into her again.

Almost against her will, she slammed her thighs together, trapping his hand.

"Doesn't that feel good, sweetheart?" he asked. "Do you want me to stop?"

"No. Yes." She couldn't think straight. Her breathing had run off course.

"Relax. Okay?" He shook his hand, as if asking her to loosen her grip. "I won't hurt you."

"I know." She sank back, only then realizing that in her excitement, she'd pushed herself up. Against every instinct she possessed, she allowed her thighs to part for him.

"That's it," he murmured, brushing his lips over her ear. He kissed the sensitive area below her lobe, and then trailed his tongue along her jawline and nipped her chin.

In the next second, his mouth covered hers. He pushed his tongue past the seam of her lips and swept the inside of her cheek, the roof of her mouth and mated with her tongue. Her insides quivered with longing, quaked with a need for something she couldn't name. When he abandoned her mouth, and kissed a path to her breasts, she boldly fisted his hair and drew him closer, arching her back when he lightly bit her nipple.

"Sit on top of me," he said raggedly, inserting his fingers deeper into her slick wetness.

He rubbed something, down there, that made her jerk.

"Can you do that?" he asked, touching her again, and sending a ripple of pleasure through her body.

She struggled to recall what they were talking about, getting frustrated when he suddenly withdrew his hand.

"Listen to me, sweetheart. I want you to sit on top of me."

She blinked blearily at him, unable to move or think beyond the moment. Then he grasped her hips and urged her to lift herself off the mattress. She followed his lead, waiting until he positioned himself in the center of the bed, tensing when he encouraged her to swing one leg over his body. She felt horribly exposed, nothing guarding her womanhood but a triangle of blond hair.

Her only solace was that he kept his gaze upward, roaming her face, her breasts. And then he looked there. Instinctively she used her hands to cover herself.

Jake smiled gently, and kneaded her breasts, shifting his attention to her achingly rigid nipples. She glanced down at his manhood, swollen and hard, straining toward her. She couldn't help herself, she had to touch him again. Lightly at first, and then she slid the palm of her hand down the side of his shaft, spreading the moisture that had beaded on the tip.

He moaned slightly. "That feels good," he said, reaching behind and squeezing her buttocks. "See? That's all I want to do. Touch you and look at you, just like you're doing to me."

Her unfairness to him struck her. He'd readily exposed himself to her. This was Jake, she reminded herself. He didn't want to hurt her. In just a matter of minutes, he'd made her feel better than she'd ever felt in her life. Yet she'd been married, been bedded many, many times in the beginning. After the first year, the shock had worn off and she'd acknowledged that Running Bear was her protector and that by Comanche standards, he'd treated her kindly so she hadn't even minded. So why was this different? Why hadn't Running Bear made her body thrum to life like this?

"Rebecca?"

She moved her hand, nervously sucking in a breath, getting used to the idea that he could see almost everything. What was still hidden from him, he quickly remedied. Her heart nearly stopped when he reached between her legs and spread her nether lips. She almost jumped off him, but was suddenly distracted by the wild leap of his manhood. And then he found that spot again, that sensitive little nub, and she closed her eyes and strained against his thumb.

He rubbed slowly, and then quickened the motion until she thought her skin would burst from her body. A startled cry crawled up her throat. She had no idea what was happening. A heated flush gushed from the pit of her belly up to her chest as if she'd gotten too close to the fire. She jerked once, twice, uncontrollably, and bent over to clutch his shoulders.

With gentle force, he pushed her back upright with his free hand kneading her breast. "That's it."

She whimpered when another spasm hit. "I don't know what's happening."

Surprise registered in his eyes, and then he smiled. "Trust me."

Trust him? She couldn't think right now. She could only...

The contractions came faster, the sensation between her thighs almost unbearable, the fever raging through her body terrifyingly unfamiliar. She tried to shove him away, but then went limp, suddenly lost in the pleasure of it all. When Jake started to withdraw his hand, she shamelessly pulled him back.

He shook free, and gripped her hips. "Lift up," he told her in a hoarse voice. "Come on."

She let him guide her, but was too dazed to understand what he was doing until she felt the blunt head of his manhood nudge her opening. Her muscles involuntarily clenched. His fingers dug slightly into her flesh as she let him pull her down on him.

"You're so small and tight," he said raggedly. "We'll go slow."

She wished she had something to hold on to, but she didn't dare get near his ribs. Clenching her teeth and fisting her hands, she slowly sank down, ordering herself not to tense as he filled her.

Jake's eyes briefly drifted closed and he groaned low in his throat. "That's it." He moved his hands from her hips to her breasts and again gently kneaded.

Finally, she'd sunk down as far as she could, awed by how completely he'd consumed her. She wiggled to get into a more comfortable position, and he groaned again. At first she'd thought she hurt him, but he moved his hips, asking for more. She experimented, moving back and forth, but then repeated the motion of sliding onto him and retreating.

That seemed to please him the most, and he took her by the hips again, controlling the rhythm, up and down, going slow at first, and then faster and faster.

She caught on quickly because the sensation felt good to her, too. Bending her knees more, she pushed herself up as far as she could without losing him, and then came down hard, taking as much of him in as she could.

Jake moaned, the sound almost feral, like something she would hear coming off the mountains at midnight while huddled in her teepee. His eyes mere slits, he found her breasts once more, and lifted his hips, hard, fast, until her buttocks slapped against him. He arched into her, his face a tense mask, his jaw clenched. His chest heaved, a strangled cry escaped his lips and then he went limp beneath her.

For a minute, his hands stilled at her breasts, and then as he opened his eyes wider, his mouth curved in a satisfied smile that made her grow warm once more.

"That was—awesome," he said, breathing in deeply and exhaling slowly.

"What does this word mean?"

Chuckling, he teased her nipple until it ached. Then he curled up and soothed it with his tongue. When he slowly lay back down, she could tell by his grim expression that lifting up like that had hurt his side.

She swung off him, ignoring his protest, and snuggled beside him, careful not to press against his ribs. But he foolishly lifted his arm and pulled her closer. She didn't fight him because the action would only cause him further pain.

Besides, if she let him continue to play with her nipples, she'd want to start over, and she didn't think he was ready to mate again.

"Tell me what awesome means," she said, partly to distract him, and partly because she truly wanted to know. She'd always read a lot and was proud of her wide vocabulary, but sometimes he used words she didn't understand.

He stretched out his free arm and grinned at the ceiling. "Where I come from, it's a highly overused word of the moment, though starting to die out. That and perfect storm."

There he went with that frustrating speech again. "A storm is never perfect. They're scary."

He made a funny expression, and then his face got so serious it made her skin tingle. But not in a good way. He sighed and rubbed his eyes. "I have something to tell you," he said, tightening his arm around her, almost too tight and stoking a spark of fear in her belly. "It's about where I come from."

15

REBECCA HATED the way Jake had tensed, his mouth pulling into a straight line. She suddenly felt uncomfortable being naked beside him, and didn't like that she had to pry his arm from around her waist so that she could reach the coverlet folded back at the foot of the bed.

"I thought you were leaving," he said, looking relieved when she pulled the quilt over them.

"You said you have something to tell me."

"I do." He sighed. "I warn you, though, it's going to sound crazy."

"Tell me," she prompted, when he stayed silent too long.

"You've been talking about the railroad men coming. Have you seen a train?"

"Yes, many times. I rode on them when I was a child."

"Okay, not a good example." Jake rubbed the top of his head, frowning. "What about the telegraph? Isn't it amazing that you can send a message practically through the air?"

She nodded, apprehension niggling at her as she studied the nervous tic at his jaw.

"What I'm trying to say is that new things are discovered all the time, things we would never have dreamed possible until they suddenly existed. Would you agree?"

"Yes." She pulled the quilt more tightly to her breasts, trying to understand his suddenly strange mood. The moon wasn't full.

"Keep that in mind when I tell you this." He paused, cupping one hand over her cheek, his blue eyes piercing in their intensity, and feeding her uneasiness. "When I said I'm not from around here— There's no good way to say this. I'm not from this time. I live in the future."

Wordlessly, she stared back at him, helpless to understand what he was saying. It made no sense.

"I know it sounds crazy, and I know you think this has something to do with my hitting my head. I did too at first. But it's been almost a week, and believe me, I don't have that good an imagination."

Rebecca swallowed. "I don't understand. You're here now. The future is not until tomorrow or next week or next year..."

"Or a hundred and forty years from now." He continued to hold her gaze, his eyes imploring her to ponder his meaning.

She shrank from him, her body numb with worry and fear. Doc Davis had thought Jake was all right. What would he say if he heard such a fanciful tale?

"Oh, God, don't. Please." Jake rubbed her shoulder. "I've dreaded telling you. I knew you wouldn't understand. Something happened out in the desert where Slow Jim found me. Somehow I crossed a time barrier. I'm guessing at this, but that's why I need to know the exact spot where he found me."

Thoughts flew through her head like a flock of birds rushing south for the winter. His strange speech pattern, words he used that she didn't understand, his calm acceptance of her past... "This future you speak of, how is it different from now?"

"That's a tough one. There are a lot more conveniences in the kitchen for instance, and we don't use fire to heat our homes. Transportation, communication, that's all different."

She listened silently as he described inventions that she had trouble understanding. Sometimes he went into so much detail that she had to believe he was telling the truth. But then she'd read a Jules Verne novel once, full of fancy. And how many times had Wind In The Trees told magical tales by the campfire on cold winter nights. Her storytelling had been so real that the children sometimes had trouble falling asleep. Was Jake nothing more than a good storyteller?

"In your world," she said finally. "You have Indians?"

He smiled. "Yes, some of them live in cities, some choose to live on reservations. They own their own property, and live alongside and marry white people if they want. We also call them Native Americans." He shrugged. "They were here first."

This sounded very strange to Rebecca. "And if a white woman is bedded by—"

He found her hand under the quilt and kissed it. "None of that matters. Not to civilized people, anyway."

This made the most sense of all. She remembered Jake's reaction to finding out she'd lived with the Comanche. He hadn't even blinked. He'd been sorry she lost her husband.

"This is a lot to take in, I know." He slid a hand across her belly and pulled her close. "I need you to promise not to tell anyone, not even Kitty. I can't have Wade thinking I'm crazy, or he won't trust me."

She stiffened. "You saw how awful the Rangers are. You must stay away from them."

"I can't." Jake closed his eyes. "It's complicated, but I can't let them get away with what they've been doing."

"But you're only one man—"

The hard pounding at the door startled them both. "Malone?" It was one of the Rangers. "The captain says to get ready. We ride in fifteen minutes."

THE MOON WAS NEARLY FULL and provided the only light in front of the closed livery at the edge of town.

Jake grabbed the saddle from the railing and tossed it onto the mare's sway back, tightening the cinch quickly. He hadn't ridden in a year, and he was too sore to be sitting astride a horse for long, but he had no choice. Knowing what little he did about Wade, tonight was likely a test. Either that, or Bart here had his own plans for dealing with an interloper.

"Where's everyone else?" Jake asked him, tired of the silence since the man had summoned him from Rebecca's warm bed.

"They're coming."

As if on cue, the thundering approach of horses drew his attention toward the four riders appearing out of the darkness. Wade rode lead. Where the hell had they come from?

"Let's go." Wade galloped past them, and Jake and Bart quickly swung into their saddles.

When Bart seemed content to trail the group, Jake stayed with him. He liked bringing up the rear so that he could watch what was going on. What he didn't like was that Corbin wasn't there, which meant he was probably still in town. With Rebecca.

The thought of the bastard even looking at her, much

less touching her, drove a stake of fury straight into Jake's heart. He could only hope the guy was out cold. Which was entirely probable, Jake thought, trying to calm down. Shit, he had to get his hands on a gun.

After what seemed like an hour, they came to a fork in the road, and the horses were pulled to a stop. The four men dismounted, and each of them handed Bart their reins. "You two wait here," Wade said. "Bart, make sure no one passes."

Bart muttered something unintelligible, netting him a menacing look from Wade, and for the first time, Jake got the feeling the Ranger didn't want to be here.

"What about me?" Jake asked, his mind zigzagging as he tried to pinpoint what had given him that impression, and how he could use the information.

"Stay with Bart. Have the horses ready." Wade adjusted his hat, checked his gun.

This wasn't gonna be good. "What's going on?" Jake asked. "What are we doing out here?"

"If I wanted you to know, I reckon you wouldn't have had to ask the question," Wade said with his gun raised and aimed at Jake's face. "Isn't that right?"

Jake looked him dead in the eyes. "That reminds me. I should have a gun."

Chuckling, the captain lowered his weapon. "You got a way of tickling my funny bone, Malone."

"That's a no on the gun?"

"We'll talk about it when we get back to town," he said, all business again. "Let's go boys."

Jake watched them run toward a grove of cottonwoods, and then with the stealth of preying tigers, slipped through the trees and scrub brush, crouching when they were out in the open.

"Why didn't they take the horses?" Jake asked Bart.

He didn't answer, only tugged up the collar of his coat.

It *was* pretty damn cold, and Jake was grateful for the borrowed coat he wore even though it smelled like stale tobacco.

"Where's Corbin?"

"Drunker than shit, like always." Bart glanced over his shoulder, probably nervous that he'd spoken out of turn.

Jake decided to drop the subject of Corbin. "Too cold to be out tonight. Hope this is worth it."

Bart grunted.

"Can't we tether the horses? Why stand here like this?"

"No." Bart stared off toward the grove of trees though every one of the men had disappeared. "They won't be long."

"So what are they doing?"

"Shut up."

A yell came from the other side of the trees. Then a gunshot. More yelling. The horses whinnied and stomped their hooves. Taken by surprise, Jake almost lost hold of the roan.

"Shit." He looked at Bart. "Should we go help them?"

He snorted. "They don't need us," he said, obviously unconcerned, and put a long thin cigarette between his lips.

An eerie silence descended, and then a second gunshot split the air. A few moments later, a horse galloped out from the trees toward Jake and Bart, before it circled into the darkness.

Jake peered toward the cottonwoods, his mind racing. A gunshot, a horse with no saddle, no rider. Sweat coated the back of his neck. He'd bet anything there'd been another hanging. He saw the Rangers start to emerge from the shadows, but they didn't seem to be in a hurry.

Bart puffed on his cigarette, his face a hard mask of barely controlled repugnance, the tension radiating from his body enough to power a small cabin. Whatever had just gone down, Jake was now complicit. Had that been the plan? Was Wade that smart?

The men approached, their expressions unreadable. "Bad news," Wade announced as he calmly took the reins of his horse. "Looks like the vigilantes struck again."

Jake tamped down his anger and disgust, and glanced at Bart, hoping like hell he'd found the group's weak link.

The next evening, Jake stayed in Rebecca's room and out of the saloon. He hadn't outright complained about his ribs, but he'd subtly allowed Wade to think he was hurting, hoping Wade would prefer that Jake lie low and heal quickly. He needed time to think about how he should proceed, and he needed to gauge how Rebecca was handling what he'd told her about him being from the future. He needed to be with her.

"Tonight I will start sewing your new shirt," she said, folding the towel strips that he'd washed, and she'd dried by hanging them by the kitchen fire.

He smiled, thinking about her startled reaction when he'd insisted on doing the washing. She was even more shocked to learn that he always did his own laundry.

"No sewing tonight," he said sternly, and she abruptly turned to look at him. He waggled his eyebrows up and down. "I have other plans for you."

She got his message, tried not to smile, and shook her head in mock disapproval. "Work before pleasure."

"Says who?" He slid in behind her and pulled her back against his chest. Her hair tickled his nose. With one arm circled around her middle, he used his other hand to comb through her hair. "Come lie down with me."

She spun around in his arms, her eyes troubled. "Will the captain call for you tonight?"

"I don't think so." He hadn't relayed last night's activities. The less she knew the better. But she was curious and worse, disappointed that he'd "thrown in" with the Rangers. To explain too much could endanger them both.

"If they do, you should refuse to go. You're not well." Her thumb brushed the corner of his mouth. "Being outside in the cold wind last night has made your blister red again. I'll have to treat it." She hesitated, and he'd bet her cheeks were suddenly pinker than his healed blister. She was fishing again, like she had once before, trying to figure out where he'd gone.

He struggled to keep his game face on. By midmorning, everyone in town knew the undertaker had been sent to collect a body at a nearby ranch. Another rustler had been hanged by the vigilantes, they were told. Except Jake could tell by the downcast eyes and furtively exchanged looks that no one believed the story. Funny how the rustlers seemed to be caught regularly, someone had murmured, but there was never any sign of the cattle. Good observation.

Their gazes met and held for several long moments, and then she reached for the pouch where she kept the salve.

"I'm okay." He stilled her hand. "You must've learned to use cactus sap from your husband's people."

Rebecca smiled fondly. "Bird Song taught me many remedies that Doc Davis calls hogwash, but they often work. I've seen it with my own eyes." Sadness replaced the smile. "She's sick. None of her medicine has eased her pain. I've been reading Doc Davis's book to see if she might have a white man's disease."

He remembered her reading in those murky hours by

his bedside. If the woman did have a white man's disease, he knew what that meant. He liked that Rebecca was so caring, but glad that she wouldn't witness the woman's deterioration. "Do you miss your husband's people?"

The smile was back, in her eyes this time. "Sometimes. Bird Song was like a mother to me. But to most of the tribe I was still an outsider. You are close to your family?"

Jake shrugged, not keen on going in that direction. "My father died a few years ago. I have a sister who I rarely see."

"And your mother?"

Jake slid his hands lower and squeezed her backside, chuckling when she squealed. "I'm going to strip off your dress and then make love to you the rest of the night."

She drew back, regarding him with wide shocked eyes.

"You have a problem with that?" he asked, already tackling the row of dreaded buttons.

She started to laugh and stifled herself.

A thought occurred to him, and he shook his head at his own stupidity. He unfastened the cuffs. With them loose, the dress was big enough on her that he easily pulled it off, buttons intact. A swift yank of the drawstring that held up her bloomers, and in seconds, she stood before him naked, her nipples already beaded.

Another minute and his clothes joined hers in a heap on the floor.

They'd made love after he returned in the early hours, and again when they'd awoken midmorning. Already she'd lost some of her shyness, and didn't flinch when he turned her around and kissed the three long thin scars across her back. He reached around to cup her breasts as he ran his tongue between her shoulder blades and up to her nape.

She shivered and laughed. "That tickles."

"What about this?" Abandoning her right breast, he drew his hand down her belly, stopping just short of the V of curls.

She squirmed, wiggling her fanny against his aroused cock.

"I'm going to give you an hour to stop that."

Grinning, Rebecca turned in his arms, lifting her face for his kiss. "I like it when you tease me."

"What makes you think I'm teasing?" He forced her backward until her legs hit the bed. He laid her down, and stretched out beside her, arranging her hair so that her breasts were exposed.

He leisurely rolled his tongue over the rosy crown, pleased that she arched her back and let her thighs fall slightly apart, humbled by how much she trusted him. Even after being whipped and held captive by Comanches, treated like garbage by the Rangers, Rebecca had found it in her heart to trust him with her life, with her savaged body.

His chest nearly burst with the sudden surge of emotion welling up inside him. Sweet, brave, fragile Rebecca trusted him. Had he ever been given such a precious gift? He doubted he was worthy. God, he couldn't let her down. No matter what, he had to keep her safe, get her out of Diablo Flats. It wouldn't be easy, balancing his duty to protect the rest of the innocent people suffering from the Rangers' tyranny, and concentrating on Rebecca.

Implausibly, Jake's thoughts skipped to his father. Had it been this way for him? Having to make the hard decision between taking care of the people he'd sworn to protect and the ones he loved. Jake's heart hammered his chest. Love? Did he love Rebecca? Was it possible to feel that deeply in such a short time? What he felt right now was so unfamiliar he honestly didn't know.

She'd been his caregiver, always there when he'd opened his eyes from that morphine haze. She'd bathed his forehead with cool compresses, brought him water for his parched throat, and nursed him back from the edge of death. Was he confusing gratitude with love?

She sighed impatiently, and he smiled, transferring his attention to her other breast, nipping at her ripened nipple. He splayed his hand across her belly, felt her spasm beneath his palm, before he slid his hand lower to the juncture of her thighs. He waited, willing her to part her legs further for him, and welcome his probing fingers.

Rebecca slowly opened for him, and then lifted her upper body off the mattress and kissed his chin. An aching tenderness welled inside him. From the beginning, she'd had every reason to cover herself, to thwart his advances, but she'd freely surrendered. Did she too feel this strange breathtaking warmth that had nothing to do with sex?

He slid his hand between her thighs, but immediately knew that wasn't going to be enough. He wanted to touch her, and he wanted to pleasure her. But he also desperately needed to be inside of her.

With a deftness that startled her, he rolled over, wedging his leg between both of hers. He drew the back of his crooked finger down her flushed cheek, and gazing into her dazed greenish-blue eyes, he positioned himself over her. Moving his hand to his cock, he teased her opening, watching her eyes to make sure she was ready. "You're so beautiful," he whispered. "Too much pain. Too much sorrow. Let me make you feel good."

She inhaled sharply at his words and her eyes grew heavy with tears. She touched his shoulder, ran her hand gently down his flank, her worry clear.

"You just relax. I'm not gonna do anything stupid. I just can't—" He eased inside of her, the tight warmth stilling everything in him but pleasure and need. He wanted to thrust hard and fast, bury himself until he could forget about everything but how damn good she felt. Instead, he braced himself with a hand on either side of her head and he leaned down to capture her mouth.

She parted her lips with a tiny sob and she clutched at his back. When she pressed into him, he nearly lost his mind. He met her thrust with his own, filling her, feeling the grip of her silky heat and he moaned into her mouth, telling her with his cock, with his kiss, that if this were a dream, some crazed hallucination, he never wanted to wake up. And if she was as real as the pulse in his neck, as the feel of her heel sliding up his leg, that he would do whatever it took to keep her safe and by his side.

16

THE NEXT NIGHT, while Jake was sitting in the saloon with the captain and some of the other Rangers, Rebecca tidied up the room and washed her hair. She smiled at the pair of gray woolen socks balled up and tucked under the lip of the washbasin. She knew he tried to be neat, but his things seemed to end up in the most unexpected places. He'd admitted that in his life in the future, his living quarters, what he called an apartment, wasn't always as orderly as it should be.

As she brushed out her hair, she thought about the things like cars, microwaves, telephones and indoor showers that he'd described. Most of them frightened her. Not because she'd reckoned he was crazy and his tales a creation of his fertile mind, but because he spoke of his "modern conveniences" with such fervor that she knew he missed his life. She knew the time would come that he would return.

Oh, how she would miss him. The notion alone brought a lump to her throat and the threat of tears to her eyes. How glad it made her heart to set eyes on him, even from across a room. There was so much good in him. It showed in so many ways. He wasn't just kind to her, but he treated Kitty and the other women politely and with the respect he would a society woman. He never referred to them as whores but as ladies. Even when the other men gave him a hard time about it.

And never once when he spoke of the Comanche had he used words like filthy Indians, or savages or heathens like the Rangers and most of the other white men. To Jake, they were people, no different from the men and women who lived in town or the nearby ranches.

The way he treated her touched her heart the most. Like she was the most precious woman on earth. His protectiveness was plain enough that the Rangers stayed clear of her, even the captain hadn't said a word about using her to service the soon-to-arrive railroad men, and she hadn't missed the traces of envy in Ruby and Trixie's eyes. She loved that he touched her often and not simply because he wanted to bed her. He seemed to like playing with her hair and giving her unexpected kisses on the side of her neck, and on the palm of her hand for no reason.

The only thing that troubled her was the time he spent with the Rangers. When he rode with them in the middle of the night, and she lay in bed awake with too much time to think, she questioned whether she might be wrong about him. She hated harboring the smallest doubt, but there was no denying the truth. He knew these men were responsible for horrible acts of cruelty, and had witnessed their ghastly treatment of her. Yet he continued to ride with them, drink with them, eat with them.

Kitty told her not to worry. Jake was only doing what he had to do. Her friend had even suspected that Jake had exchanged his allegiance to Wade for Rebecca's safety. But if that were true, he could achieve the same goal by taking her away from Diablo Flats. The anxiety wouldn't let her be. For too long she had depended on someone else for her security, first her husband and Bird Song, and then Kitty, and now Jake. It was time she relied upon herself. She was much stronger than the girl who'd been captured five years ago, and she had an obligation. To help Bird Song. If only she had a horse, Rebecca was certain she could find the tribe.

The brisk knock at her door was followed by Kitty's voice. "Rebecca? We need you downstairs."

Her stomach clenched, just as it always did when she had to go to the saloon, but at least Jake would be there. She set down her brush and opened the door. Kitty was already going down the stairs. Rebecca saw why she was in such a hurry. The place was crowded, much more than usual. Nearly every table was taken and there wasn't an empty seat at the bar.

She recalled only one other busy night like this and she'd been forced to serve drinks. At least she wouldn't have to take customers upstairs like the other girls. The thought made her shudder as she hurried to find Kitty loading a tray at the end of the bar.

"There was another hanging last night," Kitty murmured under her breath. "I think the men are feeling safer sticking around town."

"Where's Jake?" Rebecca glanced around the room at some of the faces she was starting to recognize.

"He left with Bart and Vernon about half an hour ago."

Kitty added two shots of whiskey to her order and then picked up the tray. "Get rid of the long face. Wade sent him, and Jake didn't have time to run up and tell you. I told him I would."

She nodded and took Kitty's place at the bar, loading a tray with foaming mugs of beer that the mean-faced bartender slid toward her. Working quickly, she managed to skim the room, locating where each Ranger was sitting.

She spotted the captain but not Corbin, which made her nervous. Ruby was hanging over one of the card players. No sign of Lola or Trixie. Maybe he was upstairs with one of them.

"We're taking that to the kitchen," Kitty said, indicating the newly filled tray. "Lloyd, I need a bottle for Wade," she told the bartender as she hurriedly scooped up shot glasses and then led the way toward the back. "It's too crowded out here. Wade wants to talk to the boys in private."

Rebecca nodded, breathing deeply to keep herself calm. She needed to concentrate on the heavy tray that the bartender had forced her to overload. He'd been nasty to her ever since Jake had made him apologize to her and Kitty. She didn't care though. She'd carried buffalo hides uphill in the pouring rain heavy enough to make a grown white man weep. The urge to tell Lloyd just that made her smile.

When they entered the kitchen, four of the Rangers had already pulled up chairs close to the cook fire. The captain came in behind them, along with three other men Rebecca hadn't seen before. Kitty offered shot glasses, while Rebecca passed out the beer.

"Where's Corbin?" one of the Rangers asked.

Captain Wade seemed irritated. "We're starting without him."

The men exchanged knowing looks as they took off their hats and positioned their chairs. Corbin was likely too drunk again. Jake had confided to Rebecca that some of the Rangers were getting nervous because they thought Corbin was out of control. The information had made her worry more for Jake.

"What's she doing here?" the captain asked Kitty.

"I needed help carrying the trays."

"Send her back out to the saloon." He narrowed his eyes on Rebecca, and addressed her directly. "Don't go running back to your room like a goddamn scared rabbit. There are plenty of tables that need waiting on."

Normally his tone would have frightened her. This time she fought to hide her contempt for the man.

"Go," Kitty ordered in a low warning voice, and Rebecca realized that she'd stared too long at the captain.

She set down the last beer and clutching the tray to her breast, left the kitchen. She'd gotten halfway down the short hall and stopped, curious suddenly about what the Rangers were discussing. Quietly she slipped back, and listened outside the door.

KITTY POURED WHISKEY into the shot glasses, pretending disinterest in the conversation. Part of her wanted to run from the kitchen, leave them to their evil plans. She smelled trouble brewing, felt it the minute she saw the tall bulky man they called Sebastian walk into the saloon earlier. He'd come to town before, nearly two years ago. He showed no sign of recognizing her, but she hadn't forgotten him. The bastard had paid for her the entire night. He'd been crude and rough, and she'd been tempted to grab his gun out of the holster he'd hung on the bedpost and blow him to kingdom come. That is, until she saw the notches on his pistol handle.

What had hurt the most was that the gunslinger appeared to have been a friend of Wade's. She'd tried to convince herself that Wade hadn't known about the man's quirks, and for a time she believed it. But Wade was different now, she wasn't sure she knew him anymore. One thing she did know for certain, she'd either put a bullet in Sebastian's head or leave Diablo Flats tonight before she'd let him touch her again.

"What are they saying in Austin?" Wade asked Sebastian.

"Up north and back East they're paying damn near close to thirty-eight dollars a head."

"Shit." Moses grunted. "We only got five dollars a head for the last herd we drove to Dallas."

The man who'd come in with Sebastian said, "Why the hell did you sell? We coulda drove 'em to the railhead in Abilene."

"We ain't here to talk about the past," Wade cut in. "We knew we could get a better deal, but we didn't have the time or manpower. But don't you fret none, boys." He smiled. "We got another thousand head grazing northeast of town."

"By next week we expect to add another—" Moses caught Wade's threatening look and shut up.

Sebastian straightened. "You holding out on us, Captain?"

Wade gave a small shake of his head and threw a look toward Kitty. She pretended not to notice, and started refilling the shot glasses.

"The railroad men are gonna be here in a few days," Wade said. "When they ain't fighting with Houston over moving the capitol, those government fellas in Austin have been courting the Kansas Pacific. I wager we get some rails not too far from here."

Kitty could feel Sebastian's stare weighing heavy on her back. In spite of herself, she chanced a peek at him.

He smiled, his dingy tobacco-stained teeth making her queasy. "I know you. I never forget a redhead."

She shuddered, her pleading gaze finding Wade's watchful eyes.

"Better get out there, Kitty," he said. "We got more customers tonight than Lloyd and the other girls can handle."

She nodded gratefully, and left before Sebastian could

say another word to her. But she'd barely made it to the hall when she heard him ask, "Who's the young yellow-haired whore that was in here earlier? I think I might have a hankerin' for some fresh meat."

Kitty froze and listened, hoping like hell that Wade had the good sense to squash that notion. Jake wouldn't stand for any man putting his hands on Rebecca, or blood would be shed. Then she saw her, Rebecca scrambling toward the saloon. Had she been standing outside the entire time? How much had she heard? Christ Almighty, the girl had too much spunk. She was gonna get herself killed before Jake could get her out of here.

Without waiting to hear a response, Kitty hurried toward the bar. Rebecca had just picked up a tray of beer, her face pale, frightened and angry.

"You promised, no knives," Kitty whispered fiercely. "Jake should be back soon."

Rebecca said nothing, only glared at something snide Lloyd murmured, and snatched up the tray.

While Kitty watched her walk purposefully to a table, she thought for a moment, and then ran upstairs to her room. Something bad was going to happen soon, she knew. Too many folks running scared and willing to ignore their principles. She'd already figured the Rangers had something to do with the rustling because for the past two months every one of them had had too much silver in their pockets. But now it sickened her to consider they were responsible for the hangings, too.

She'd tried to separate Wade from the rest of them, tried to convince herself that he'd been unaware of any wrongdoing. What a fool she'd been. The men wouldn't think of crossing their captain. Out of respect, out of fear, it didn't matter, they simply wouldn't do anything without his consent.

How could Wade have sunk so low? He'd been a good lawman once. He'd been her hero.

With a heavy heart, she opened the dresser drawer and rifled through her underthings until she felt the smooth leather case that sheathed her dagger. Ironically, Wade had given her the small pearl-handled knife for protection eight years ago. She never dreamed she'd need it. Not with him around.

Lifting her skirt, she slipped the dagger under the top of her stockings. It felt heavy against her leg, and she prayed she wouldn't lose it. She smoothed down her dress, checked her bodice and then peered into the mirror that she had propped up on the dresser. Her reflection startled her. When had she gotten so damn old? Lines fanned out from her eyes and she found a tiny new wrinkle at the right corner of her red tinted mouth.

She knew the other girls thought she was lying about her age, and it hurt to see them whisper, to see the lofty smiles curve their youthful lips. Sadly, she hadn't lied. She'd just turned thirty in the fall, which meant she'd spent exactly half her life as a whore. It was too late for her. But not for Rebecca, and Kitty had made her a promise she meant to keep.

She started to turn for the door, but caught a last look at her weary made-up face. Oh, what she wouldn't do for another chance at life. Kitty sighed. If only there were a God…

IT WAS ALMOST DAWN when Jake slipped into Rebecca's room and saw her lying in bed, curled up on her side. He was annoyed that the door was unlocked, anyone could have walked in. But he knew she'd been waiting for him to return, and she seemed fine, and that's all that mattered.

Quietly he slid off his boots and unbuckled his belt. He

was so damn tired he was amazed he'd made it back to town without falling asleep in the saddle. The only thing that kept him awake was soreness. His head no longer ached, but it wasn't easy sitting on a horse for as many hours as he'd been doing lately. But then he figured it was good practice. Within the next couple of days, he was going to have to ride to Austin.

And hope like hell it wasn't a mistake.

Not that he had much of a choice. He was hoping he had more time to build a case, prove that the massive herd of cattle grazing east of Otis Sanford's land had been rustled by the Rangers. But if he didn't find someone in authority to help stop them soon, the cattle would be shipped north and the town undertaker would be building a lot more pine boxes.

His biggest problem was who he could trust. Or for that matter, how to find out who had jurisdiction over Captain Wade and his men. The law was a mystery to him here. If he left Texas in search of a federal marshal, he could waste a whole lot of time just to discover that the man had no authority over the Rangers.

Jake decided it made sense to go to the capitol. He'd skip the big Ranger office located there, since he couldn't assume there wasn't collaboration between the Rangers there and Wade, and instead find a judge who could guide him. Too bad Rebecca didn't know the ins and outs of Texas law. But she'd been little more than a kid when she'd been taken.

The reminder of her capture was like a knife being driven into his heart. It had required all of his willpower not to show how he felt about the man who'd inflicted those scars on her back. Beat with a whip because she'd tried to run away, had dared to defy him in front of his people. Jake understood it was the custom and mores of the 1800s

Comanche, but it grated on him far more than he'd ever let Rebecca know. The last thing she needed was to feel guilty for marrying Running Bear and doing what she needed to do to survive.

He shrugged out of his shirt, and peeled off his jeans, smiling when Rebecca snuggled deeper under the quilt, her face at peace in sleep. Damn, he wished he knew how much he could trust Kitty. Knowing her, she probably had all the answers for him, but he couldn't risk confiding in her. He believed she genuinely wanted Rebecca safe and out of Diablo Flats, but he knew she had this thing with Wade. When it came down to it, who would she choose?

As much as Jake hated to disturb her, he couldn't stand the thought of trying to sleep without her cheek pressed to his chest. He gently rolled back the quilt, and she turned her head and blinked at him. A sweet smile lifted her lips.

"Hey," he said, sliding in beside her. "I missed you."

She threw an arm around his waist and sighed. "I hate it when you're away."

He briefly closed his eyes, dreading when he'd have to tell her he was leaving. He only hoped he could make her understand that for her, staying would be safer than going with him. If he were caught, he'd be shot or hanged. She'd be left defenseless, to be brutalized and killed. He ruthlessly shoved the thought aside before it clouded his judgment.

"I'm sorry I couldn't tell you I was going." He kissed her hair. "It all happened quickly."

"Kitty told me. Where were you?"

He was surprised by the question. They never talked about the Rangers' business. But it was the perfect opening. She had to understand the gravity of the problem the town faced. "I'm going to tell you something about the Rangers that you can't repeat, not even to Kitty. Or it could get us both killed."

She drew back to stare at him, the muted dawn light filtering through the window to show her face. She didn't seem frightened, maybe a bit wary, but he already knew she was tough.

"Last night I was sent to check on a herd of cattle and round up strays. I'm pretty sure all the cattle had been rustled. They had different brands." He paused, confused by her lack of surprise. "Do you know what that means?"

"The Rangers are the rustlers."

He studied her face. "You already knew?"

She gave a small shrug. "They're bad men. They leave town to look for the rustlers but they never find any."

"Smart lady." He smiled. "I have a feeling the rest of the town may be starting to get the hint."

She nodded solemnly. "And the vigilantes?"

He hadn't wanted to go there. "I don't know. When people get nervous, they do things out of fear they often regret."

"Did Corbin kill Mr. Otis so he wouldn't talk?" she asked softly.

He wanted to lie, tell her that the Rangers wouldn't go as far as murder. But he had a feeling she'd see right through him. "I think so, but we can't prove it."

"He had scratches on his face."

"Which could have come from you."

She stared silently at the ceiling.

"The Rangers are planning to drive the herd north but they're waiting for extra men."

She frowned. "Three strangers showed up tonight. Captain Wade knew one of them."

"Damn. That was sooner than I expected, though they're

going to need more than three men. You hear them say anything about more coming?"

Rebecca's lips parted, as if she were going to say something, but then shook her head. Finally, she looked at him with pleading eyes. "We need to leave here, Jake. Tonight."

"Ah, sweetheart. I can't do that."

"Don't you see? If they find out you know about them, they'll hurt you." She clutched his arm, her short jagged nails digging into his skin. "Oh, Jake, they'll kill you."

"If I don't stop them, more people will be killed."

She gaped at him. "How can you stop them? You can't. They're greedy and there's too much money involved and—" She bit her lip, and looked away.

He didn't like the suspicious feeling crawling up his spine. "Is there something you need to tell me?"

"No. I just don't want you to do anything foolish."

"I have a duty to stop them." He'd thought long and hard tonight while trying to stay awake in the saddle about how much to admit to her at this point. Still not sure he was doing the right thing, he reached for the jeans he'd discarded, and dug into his pocket for his wallet. He knew she hadn't seen it, nor apparently had anyone else while he was out cold because if they had, he would've had a lot more explaining to do before now. "I have something to show you."

He flipped open the brown leather trifold, pausing to gauge her reaction before revealing his badge.

Rebecca blinked, and then her eyes widened to the size of silver dollars. Except for the words *Department of Public Safety*, there was no mistaking the star that Rangers had worn for over a hundred and seventy years. "This is— you?" she asked incredulously.

He nodded, his heart sinking at the look of horrified

betrayal on her face. She shifted, subtly shrinking away, as if she no longer trusted him.

"Where I come from, the Texas Rangers aren't like Wade and the others. They're, we're, decent men, trying to uphold the law. I swear to you, Rebecca. I'm not one of them. But I am a Ranger. That's all I know. It's all I've ever wanted to be. I need to stop these men from killing more innocent people. It's not just my job, can you understand that? It's my duty."

"Is it your duty to die? You don't even have a gun."

"Please, sweetheart. Don't worry about me. I've got a plan. I've thought about it every night, every moment I was away from you. What I need is for you to trust me. Do you think you can do that?"

The way she looked at him made his stomach clench. So much hope and fear were in her eyes. But there was also strength. The kind of strength that had kept her alive through nightmares that would have crippled most people. She touched the side of his face with her soft fingers. "I will," she said. "I do."

17

THE NEXT MORNING, from her window, Rebecca watched Slow Jim ride into town. The Rangers were expecting the half-breed, and Captain Wade had already agreed that the scout would show Jake the place where he'd been found. Wade thought Jake wanted to search the area for his belongings. Only she knew his true mission was to find the time portal, and then head to Austin before anyone had figured out that he was gone.

She still didn't understand the exact nature of this passage through time that he'd tried to explain. Sometimes Jake seemed as confused as she did.

There was a brief knock at the door before she heard it open. She knew it was Jake returning from the kitchen, even before she turned around to find him with a cup of steaming coffee in his hand. He smiled gently and passed her the brew.

She tried to smile back, but couldn't, and reckoned that it was enough that she hadn't burst into tears. "Thank you," she said, accepting the cup with a trembling hand.

"Ah, Rebecca—"

She turned away to set the cup on the stool, afraid to

put anything in her queasy stomach, afraid to look at him and let him see the misery in her heart.

He slid his arms around her waist and drew her back to his chest. "I wish there was another way."

She squeezed her eyes shut. "You could take me with you."

"You know I can't. It wouldn't be safe for you. If the Rangers caught up to us—" He sighed, and kissed the side of her neck. "I talked to Kitty. You'll be safer with her."

Rebecca stepped out of his arms and spun to look at him. "What did you tell her?"

He looked grim. "Nothing about Austin. Just that I had some business to take care of so that we'd be able to leave. She has a soft spot for you, sweetheart. She really wants to make sure you get out of Diablo Flats."

Guilt washed over her. If she told him what she'd heard last night it would confirm his suspicions. Then he'd go to Austin for sure. She wasn't convinced that she was better off staying behind. But she wouldn't beg, either. This could be Jake's way of letting her down easy. She believed that he wanted to stop the Rangers from hurting anyone else, but despite her promise to him, she didn't completely trust that he'd come back to her. Austin was far away, a big city, and she was only an Indian's whore. Or maybe he planned on going back to his other life through the time portal. Why wouldn't he? There was nothing here worth fighting for. The idea of being without him chilled her to the bone. But she'd better get used to it.

She looked at the misgiving in his beautiful blue eyes, and swallowed hard. She loved him, she realized, but not until this second had she understood the depth of her feelings for him. Loved him enough to want him safe and far from here. "If you don't come back it's all right. I wanted you to know that."

"No." He gripped her upper arms. "I'm coming back. As long as I've got breath in my body, I'll keep you safe."

Rebecca flinched, the sudden thought of Jake lifeless, dead on the ground, more than she could bear.

"I'm sorry." He wrapped his arms around her and held her tight. "I'm so sorry. I shouldn't have said that. I was trying to make a point that I would never desert you. Please tell me you understand that I'm coming back for you."

She nodded, too numb to do anything else.

He held her face in his hands. "Look at me," he said, when lifting her lashes seemed too great an effort. "I'll be gone for about five days, maybe six. Wade has business east of town. He'll be taking a few of the Rangers with him and they'll be away at least overnight, maybe longer. Kitty will get you out to Otis's ranch. You hide there until I return." He searched her eyes. "Do you understand?"

"Yes," she replied, shaken.

"I couldn't stand it if anything happened to you," he said, his voice thick. "Promise me you'll stay with Kitty."

Rebecca forced a smile. "Go. I'll be all right."

Someone knocked at the door. It was Kitty. It was time for Jake to go.

"MANY SPIRITS EXIST HERE." Eyeing him apprehensively, Slow Jim reined in his gelding at the edge of the clearing. The horse stepped sideways, threw back his head and whinnied, as if in agreement. "There," the man said, pointing to a boulder the size of a compact car. "That is where I found you."

Jake stared at the outcropping nestled against a thicket of scrub oak. Blood spattered the smoother side of the rock. His blood, presumably, which supported Slow Jim's claim that this was the exact spot. Jake quickly surveyed the area, but saw no other signs of blood. That didn't mean he hadn't crawled from somewhere else, but this was as much as he had to go on.

"Was I lying down?"

Slow Jim turned to him, his tanned face creased in a frown. "Yes."

Once again Jake was struck by the man's uncanny resemblance to Jake's friend Tom Parker. Like Slow Jim, Tom was half Comanche, and except for the long black hair and about ten pounds, the men could've been twins. It was damn eerie. Another sign that this was Jake's fate? At this point, he only cared that the man stayed as tight-lipped when he returned to town as he had on the ride out here. Though he wasn't too worried. Slow Jim sometimes worked for Wade, but Jake got the impression that he wasn't exactly a fan.

"Did I say anything when you found me?" Jake asked, as he swung down from his horse.

"No."

Something in the older man's voice made Jake ask, "Am I the first man you've found here?"

Slow Jim closed his eyes for a long moment and when he looked back, it was with weary resignation. "No. I told you. Many spirits."

"Do they go back where they came from? These other spirits?"

Slow Jim stared at the boulder for a long time, and just when Jake had given up on an answer, he said, "I haven't seen it. But there are stories. Spirits moving back and forth. I don't know if there's any truth to it."

"But there are stories."

"It's not good to be here. You should leave."

Jake hesitated, his gaze going once again to the spot beside the boulder. Slow Jim was right. He shouldn't be messing with things he didn't understand. At least not now. If he were to suddenly be sucked back into the future… Without Rebecca? What if he couldn't take her with him?

The mere thought had more impact than if the earth had quaked beneath his feet. Fisting the reins tighter, he glanced at Slow Jim. "Thanks for showing me how to get here. I'll find my way back."

The man studied him for a few seconds, shrugged his shoulders then wheeled his horse toward town.

Not daring to move toward the boulder, Jake stood for a good five minutes before he mounted, thinking about the others who had traveled here. Had they come from a distant past? A future he couldn't comprehend? Was it all an accident, a wrong step, or were those who traveled meant to? It was all so crazy he had to shake himself to get his mind right again.

The ride out had taken about half an hour. He'd paid close attention to landmarks and he was certain he could find the place later. When Rebecca was with him.

He'd purposely been trying to keep her from his thoughts. He had to stay focused. According to Kitty, there was only one way to Austin and, in her words, he'd have to be a damn fool to get lost. She'd given him specific directions, even though he'd refused to admit that that's where he was headed. He didn't believe that Rebecca had confided in her friend because she understood the stakes were too high to take that chance. He guessed that Kitty had seen the proverbial writing on the wall, and she was a smart one. The good thing was, her giving him directions to Austin told him he was right to be heading there. No matter, he trusted her to keep Rebecca safe.

Something he'd promised to do.

Shit. He couldn't go there. Rebecca was fine. He had to believe that. Too many lives depended on him. He'd taken an oath, one he held close to his heart.

He dug his heels in and flicked the reins.

Two HOURS AFTER Jake had left town, Rebecca sat on Kitty's bed and watched her dig through her dresser drawer.

"You'll need a coat." Kitty pulled out a pair of men's wool socks that had been rolled into a big thick ball. "I saw one at the general store last week. It'll be big on you but it'll do the trick."

Still numb, she watched her friend find the opening and then reach inside the sock. Kitty withdrew a fistful of silver coins and gold pieces, and then looked over with a satisfied smile. As soon as she met Rebecca's eyes, her lips drooped.

"You better stop your moping. We have things to do before I can get you out of town." Kitty went to the window for a quick look outside. "Wade and two of the boys left a half hour ago. I don't know where Corbin is. That's the problem."

"Kitty, I can't take your money. I don't want you to get in trouble because of me."

"Damn it, Rebecca. Don't give me a hard time. I promised Jake I'd take care of you and—"

"Don't." She wanted to cover her ears, hearing his name was too painful. "If he was worried, he wouldn't have left me."

"Oh, honey, he didn't want to leave you." Kitty dropped the money on the dresser and sat beside Rebecca. "He's coming back, you'll see."

"I don't believe he is," she whispered, the word *dead* echoing in her head.

Kitty gasped. "Don't say such a thing. Do you think he'd abandon you? He's not like the rest of them, Rebecca. You have to know that by now."

She stared down at her hands. She'd already suffered too much loss. First, her parents and her brother, and then even Running Bear. Though he hadn't been a husband of her choosing, he had not been unkind and kept her safe as he had vowed to do.

"Rebecca." Kitty shook her arm. "Listen to your heart. You know your man will be back. For goodness' sakes, he's already shown you that he's honorable—"

"And it's going to get him killed." Her voice cracked, and she stared at her hands again. "Jake is only one man. He can't go up against the captain and—" She realized what she'd said and threw Kitty an apologetic look.

"Don't worry." Kitty sighed. "I've taken off my blinders." Her chin quivered. "I wish you could've known Wade in the old days. He was a different man...."

"I'm sorry."

Kitty shrugged. "Jake is too smart to go up against Wade and the others alone. My guess is that he's getting help in Austin."

"And if the men there don't listen? Jake is a stranger to them. They know the captain and—" She saw the concern in Kitty's eyes, and understood that her friend had come to the same conclusion. Of course she didn't know about Jake being from the future, but the men in Austin might assume he was a greenhorn from the East and not take him seriously.

"He'll make them understand, honey. Jake is smart, and he has a way with words."

Rebecca swallowed and pushed to her feet. "I can tell them what I heard the other night."

Kitty's eyes darkened with fear. "What are you saying?"

"I'm going to need that coat. A horse and knife, too." She'd been selfish not to tell Jake what she'd overheard. She knew he would act on the information, but she'd wanted him to take her away and help her find Bird Song.

"Rebecca, this is madness."

"I'm a good rider and I know the terrain better than he does." Rebecca tied her hair back, her mind racing ahead. Jake would be furious, but she didn't care. Her father's ego and stubbornness had gotten her family killed. The same flaws had put Running Bear into the ground. She wouldn't stand for a man's stupidity, not anymore. "Will you help me?"

Kitty nodded haltingly, her wretched expression squeezing Rebecca's heart.

"You could come with me. Stay in Austin and make a new start."

Kitty snorted. "Honey, I can't ride a horse worth spit." She shoved some coins into Rebecca's hand, and then picked up her bundled cloak. She stood over the bed and lifted one corner of the garment. It unfurled and with a soft thud, Rebecca saw one of Cook's big kitchen knives land on the quilt. "I have a horse from Otis Sanford's ranch at the livery. It'll take me a while to get a saddle, though."

Rebecca smiled. "I only know how to ride bareback."

"Ah, yes." Kitty bit her lower lip, her eyes beginning to fill with tears.

It was hard to witness. Nothing ever made Kitty cry. Rebecca slid her arms around her and hugged her fiercely. "Go to Mr. Otis's ranch. Don't stay here."

"I just might do that."

Rebecca pulled back. "Please, Kitty. You're so certain Jake will return. Promise you'll wait for us there."

"Go get what you need from your room." Kitty handed her the knife. "I'll meet you in the alley next to the livery with some food and a canteen."

Rebecca hid the knife in the folds of her skirt until she

could properly sheathe it. Nodding, she moved backward, sadly aware that her friend had not made her a promise.

WITH NO CLOAK and only a wool shawl drawn tightly around her shoulders, Kitty stood shivering as she watched Rebecca ride out of town. There hadn't been time to buy her a coat. Kitty hoped the cloak would be warm enough until Rebecca got to Austin. Oh, God, she prayed she made it. From what Kitty could tell, she was a good rider, better than some of the men. Fast, too. She had to be fast if she wanted to catch up to Jake before dark. The idea of Rebecca spending the night alone in the desert made Kitty shiver again.

Or maybe it was the persistent feeling that she was being watched that made her tremble. She glanced over her shoulder, and then toward the doors of the saloon, checking the boardwalk in front of the boardinghouse and the general store. No one was around. Not on this cold, miserable, overcast day.

She dabbed at her eyes, and smoothed back her upswept hair, preparing to return to the saloon. It would be a while before Rebecca was missed. Hopefully long enough for Kitty to pull herself together.

As soon as she turned around, she saw him.

Corbin stepped out of the alley by the smokehouse, his mouth twisted in an evil grin. "I thought that was you riding out of town just now."

Kitty's heart thumped. Did he know that had been Rebecca? In spite of herself, Kitty glanced down the empty street, even though she knew her friend was long gone.

Without saying a word, she rushed past him toward the saloon. But he caught her arm, digging his fingers in until she cried out in pain.

"Let me go, you stupid bastard, or I'll tell Wade."

Corbin pinned her with an icy glare as he gave a short

derisive laugh. "All of it? Like how you helped the Indian whore escape?"

"I don't know what you're talking about." She jerked away from him, her legs trembling so badly she didn't think she'd make it up the boardwalk steps.

"Go ahead, run back to the saloon. I'm done with you. Wade will be, too, after I tell him what you done. Shoulda taken care of you when I did old Otis." His laughter started to fade, yet she hadn't gotten that far away from him.

She stopped, and turned. He was headed toward the livery.

A surge of fear and anger coursed through her veins. Just as she thought, he was the one who killed Otis, and now he was going after Rebecca. She lifted the hem of her skirt and ran. Just before she entered the livery, she pulled her dagger from her stocking. He stumbled on his way to his saddle, still laughing to himself.

She moved quietly and quickly, never more sure of anything she'd ever done. This bastard wasn't going to find Rebecca. And he wasn't going to talk to Wade. Not ever again. He tripped as he twisted around to look at her.

She looked right into his shocked eyes as she plunged the blade into his chest.

JAKE SPOTTED THE STREAM and knew it was time to stop. His horse needed watering and he needed a pull from the canteen himself. He squinted up at the sun, estimating that it was between twelve and one. Man, he missed his watch.

He missed Rebecca.

Crazy, because he'd seen her just a few hours ago. Dammit, he needed to keep his focus. He had to stop thinking about Rebecca. Any distraction would mean more time she was on her own. More time for Wade to find her. The smart thing, the only thing, he should be thinking about was completing this mission. He'd sworn to keep her safe, and he wasn't about to break that promise.

Impatient, he watched the chestnut drink. Jake couldn't rush the animal. Hell, he didn't know when they'd find the next watering hole. Shading his eyes, he squinted at the horizon. Too bad it got dark so early.

He wondered what Rebecca was doing. Had they made it to Otis's ranch yet? He plowed a hand through his hair, slowly, thoughtfully, something he'd seen his father do hundreds of times. Funny, Jake hadn't realized they shared that habit. Made him wonder what else he'd picked up from his old man. Dedication to the job, certainly.

The chestnut seemed like he was never going to stop drinking, and Jake grunted, realizing that impatience was something else he and his father had in common. Except when Jake worked undercover. As long as he was on the job, he could bide his time. The end result was all that mattered.

His thoughts drifted to his mother, and it occurred to him that he'd been gone for over a week, and anyone looking for him would think he'd dropped off the face of the earth. Which he sort of had. But he was officially on vacation, so no one would be wondering about him. Certainly not his mother. Since he'd just seen her on Christmas morning they were good for another four months.

Guilt took a stab at him. She'd looked terrible, and he had a feeling her drinking had reached the next level. He'd thought about bringing it up to his sister. The two of them could discuss whether they should step in…. Nah, she wouldn't give a damn. Hell, he was one to talk. What had he done?

Besides stay away more.

Just like his father had done.

The painful realization went straight for the jugular. Had he become the thing he'd despised most about his father? When had he started pushing everyone away? When had the job become his priority to the exclusion of his family? He'd even gone out on a limb to get confidential informants into rehab, but he'd done nothing to help his own mother.

He'd always admired the job his father had done as a Ranger, but as a husband and father, the man had been a disaster. Was that the kind of man Jake wanted to be?

Was it too late? Jesus, he'd left Rebecca. What the hell was wrong with him? He loved her, and he'd left her behind without knowing for certain that she would be safe. What kind of man did that? If anything happened to her...

The horse was done drinking and Jake was through saving everyone on the planet but the people that mattered the most. He filled up his canteen in a wet rush, then mounted, turning back toward Diablo Flats, racing as if his life depended on it.

SHE LAY LOW on the horse, keeping her body pressed against the warmth, not thinking about the whipping wind that burned her flesh. Every hoofbeat was another second closer to Jake. Rebecca knew she should slow down, look for signs of his passing, make sure she was on the right path, but there was a panic inside her that wouldn't listen to reason. What if her selfishness cost him his life? Kitty's life? If only she'd truly trusted him. He'd shown her in so many ways that he was a good man.

She sat up as the horse pushed faster. The wind was unbearable, but she knew the tired horse would only be tempted by water. It couldn't be that far now, and she'd have to stop. Then she could check the parched ground, look for broken branches and, with any luck, boot prints.

It was another jerk by the thirsty horse that made her

look to her right. To see another horse racing so fast there was dust flying behind him like a cape.

Her heart nearly beat out of her chest. Jake? He had turned back. Was he being chased? Had Wade discovered his plan? She pulled the reins sharply, leading her horse to a rocky bank. It wasn't tall enough to hide them, but if there was someone after Jake, she'd see them before they saw her. She'd cut them off, make them follow her away from him.

Her breath and the horse's were loud in the late afternoon sun, but she stayed still as a stone as she watched behind Jake, looking for dust. By the time she could hear the hoofbeats echo off the rocks, she was sure that no one was after him.

She urged her horse forward, faster, surer as Jake came nearer. She didn't care that she could barely feel her hands or her nose. Nothing mattered but the moment he jerked up, nearly causing his mount to throw him. He'd seen her.

It felt like forever until she could see his face, make out his smile, and then she pulled back the reins and jumped off before the horse had stopped. Then she was in strong arms, lifted from the ground.

"What the hell are you doing here?" he said, right before he kissed her so she couldn't speak.

Finally, he took a breath, and she touched his face with her cold hands, pushed at him to let her down. "I heard the Rangers talking," she said. "I should have told you. I said I trusted you, but then I didn't tell you."

"It's okay," he said. He took a step back and took off his coat, wrapping it around her shoulders. "It's okay. The only thing that matters is that you're all right. I shouldn't have left you there. I was a damn fool."

"No, it was me. I should have come with you. I heard them talking and I know what they're planning. No one in

Austin will know I was with the Comanche. They'll believe me."

He put his hands inside the coat, around her waist. "I was so afraid I'd lost you. I don't care about the Rangers or the cattle. I love you, Rebecca. I love you like I've never loved another soul. I turned back because of you."

She closed her eyes, willing the tears to stay back. Hearing him say those words felt like every hope she'd never dared dream. "I love you, Jake. But your honor and your duty is who you are. We can go together. We'll ride into Austin and make them believe us."

He smiled and kissed her again, long and slow, as if he was proving something. While she wouldn't complain, he had nothing to prove to her at all.

IT WAS BITTERLY COLD, and as soon as the horses were watered, they made camp somewhere more protected from the wind. As they sat by the fire, Jake heard about what Kitty had done for Rebecca, and they agreed that no matter what happened in Austin they'd go back for her. They kissed and hugged a lot but it bothered him that she hadn't asked about the time portal.

"I found the place. Slow Jim knew right where to take me," he said, waiting for her reaction. "It's a two-way street, that portal. That means I can go back."

She stiffened, and he hurried, cursing himself for being a fool. "You'll come with me. You'll like it there, I promise. You'll see such amazing things you won't believe your eyes. We'll have a home. You can read all day, if you want."

When she wouldn't relax in his arms, he leaned his head back to look at her. "I know it sounds scary, but I'll be right there with you. Always."

"I can't go," she said sadly.

"Rebecca," A lump rose in his throat. "I swear to you, I will never let anything bad happen."

"Oh, Jake." She turned around and touched a finger to his lips. "I know." She looked so sad, her eyes glistening with tears, he thought his heart was literally going to split in two. "Bird Song needs me. She was sick, but still alive when they took me. I have to find her. She was like a mother to me. I can't just walk away, not knowing if she can take care of herself."

A long breath left him as her words sunk in. She didn't want to go back with him? She'd said she loved him. It didn't make sense.

"I'm sorry. If you only knew how much I wish I could go. I—I—" Her voice broke on a sob. "Leaving and not knowing would haunt me forever."

His entire body tightened. How could he leave without Rebecca? He couldn't. There was no way. Did she not understand what it meant for him to leave while she stayed?

He looked deep into her earnest eyes and found his answer.

"I understand," he said, a second later. She was doing the right thing by the only family she had left. She was doing what he should have done from the beginning. Taken care of his family. Watched over his loved ones before they drifted away. Before there was nothing left of him but a silver star. "I do understand," he repeated. "And tell you what. We'll take care of business in Austin, then make sure Kitty's all right. And then we'll go find Bird Song. Both of us. Together."

A tear slipped from her eye. "You would do this? For me?"

He smiled, and brushed her cheek with the back of his fingers. He wasn't sure which was colder, but it didn't matter. "I think there's been enough of men making the decisions in your life. They sure as hell haven't done a very good job. So this time, we'll do it your way. After that," he said, winking, "it's up for negotiation."

It took a minute for the smile to lift her lips. But when she threw herself back into his arms, he had no doubt at all that this was right. Whether it was the eighteen hundreds or the twenty-first century, they belonged together. They belonged to each other.

Seven days later

THEY FOUND KITTY hiding in Otis's barn. She looked scared, but unhurt. Downright amazed that they'd come back. While Jake looked around the place, Rebecca helped pull hay from her mussed hair, and filled her in on their trip to Austin.

"It's gonna be crazy around here real soon," Rebecca told her. "Jake believes the law is serious about trying to clean up the Rangers, and they want to make an example of Wade's bunch." Rebecca squeezed her friend's arm. "I'm sorry."

"Me, too." Kitty shrugged, her eyes moist. "But Wade made his own bed. You two plan on sticking around?"

"We can't."

"I figured."

"You can't, either."

Kitty smiled. "There's food in the house. I ran over there after dark. I could fix you something before you go."

Rebecca linked an arm through hers as they headed out of the barn. She knew it wouldn't be easy to talk Kitty into going with them, but she wouldn't give up.

Jake was untying their horses from the front post. He'd found a third one. "Kitty, get your stuff. We gotta go."

The women ran to meet him, Rebecca's heart pounding in her chest. "What's happened?"

"I saw riders. We have to leave. Now."

Kitty's shoulders dropped. "You two, go on. I'll go back to the barn."

"No, you can't." Rebecca took her hands. "You have to come. Kitty, they'll kill you if they think you've had anything to do with us. What if they know what's coming?"

"It doesn't make a difference. I'm not running. I'm tired and I'm cold, and one place is as good as another."

Rebecca turned to Jake, begging him silently to do something. To make her understand.

He handed the reins to Rebecca. "Climb on up, sweetheart." He turned to Kitty. "There is a place that's different. Where you'll find a whole new way of life. Things you never dreamed of. All you have to do is find Slow Jim. You get to him, and you tell him I sent you. You tell him to take you to the rock. He'll know what to do."

Kitty frowned. "Hell, you are crazy."

"No," he said. "I'm saving your life. All you have to do is trust me. Can you do that?"

Rebecca went to Kitty. "You're the one who told me I could trust him. You were right. He'll save you. I promise."

Kitty looked at Rebecca, then back at Jake, the crazy man from who knows where. She'd have to be a damn fool to think there was a way out of this mess of a life. But then, she kinda liked fools. "What the hell," she said, wondering how she was gonna get on that horse. "It can't be worse than Diablo Flats."

Harlequin offers a romance for every mood!
See below for a sneak peek
from our paranormal romance line,
Silhouette® Nocturne™.
Enjoy a preview of REUNION by USA TODAY
bestselling author Lindsay McKenna.

Aella closed her eyes and sensed a distinct shift, like movement from the world around her to the unseen world.

She opened her eyes. And had a slight shock at the man standing ten feet away. He wasn't just any man. Her heart leaped and pounded. He reminded her of a fierce warrior from an ancient civilization. Incan? She wasn't sure but she felt his deep power and masculinity.

I'm Aella. Are you the guardian of this sacred site? she asked, hoping her telepathy was strong.

Fox's entire body soared with joy. Fox struggled to put his personal pleasure aside.

Greetings, Aella. I'm the assistant guardian to this sacred area. You may call me Fox. How can I be of service to you, Aella? he asked.

I'm searching for a green sphere. A legend says that the Emperor Pachacuti had seven emerald spheres created for the Emerald Key necklace. He had seven of his priestesses and priests travel the world to hide these spheres from evil forces. It is said that when all seven spheres are found, restrung and worn, that Light will return to the Earth. The fourth sphere is here, at your sacred site. Are you aware of it? Aella held her breath. She loved looking at him, especially his sensual mouth. The desire to kiss him came out of nowhere.

Fox was stunned by the request. *I know of the Emerald*

Key necklace because I served the emperor at the time it was created. However, I did not realize that one of the spheres is here.

Aella felt sad. Why? Every time she looked at Fox, her heart felt as if it would tear out of her chest. *May I stay in touch with you as I work with this site?* she asked.

Of course. Fox wanted nothing more than to be here with her. To absorb her ephemeral beauty and hear her speak once more.

Aella's spirit lifted. What *was* this strange connection between them? Her curiosity was strong, but she had more pressing matters. In the next few days, Aella knew her life would change forever. How, she had no idea....

Look for REUNION
by USA TODAY *bestselling author Lindsay McKenna,*
available April 2010, only from
Silhouette® Nocturne™.

▼ Silhouette®

SPECIAL EDITION

INTRODUCING A BRAND-NEW MINISERIES FROM *USA TODAY* BESTSELLING AUTHOR
KASEY MICHAELS

SECOND-CHANCE BRIDAL

At twenty-eight, widowed single mother Elizabeth Carstairs thinks she's left love behind forever....until she meets Will Hollingsbrook. Her sons' new baseball coach is the handsomest man she's ever seen—and the more time they spend together, the more undeniable the connection between them. But can Elizabeth leave the past behind and open her heart to a second chance at love?

FIND OUT IN
SUDDENLY A BRIDE

Available in April
wherever books are sold.

REQUEST YOUR FREE BOOKS!

2 FREE NOVELS PLUS 2 FREE GIFTS!

HARLEQUIN®

Blaze™

Red-hot reads!

HB10

HARLEQUIN *Presents*

2 Stories in 1

HER MEDITERRANEAN PLAYBOY

Sexy and dangerous—he wants you in his bed!

The sky is blue, the azure sea is crashing
against the golden sand and the sun is hot.

The conditions are perfect for
a scorching Mediterranean seduction
from two irresistible untamed playboys!

Indulge your senses with these two delicious stories

A MISTRESS AT THE ITALIAN'S COMMAND
by Melanie Milburne

ITALIAN BOSS, HOUSEKEEPER MISTRESS
by Kate Hewitt

Available April 2010 from Harlequin Presents!

www.eHarlequin.com

HP12910

OLIVIA GATES

BILLIONAIRE, M.D.

Dr. Rodrigo Valderrama has it all...
everything but the woman he's secretly
desired and despised. A woman forbidden
to him—his brother's widow.
And she's pregnant.

Cybele was injured in a plane crash
and lost her memory. All she knows is
she's falling for the doctor who has swept her
away to his estate to heal. If only the secrets
in his eyes didn't promise to tear
them forever apart.

Available March wherever you buy books.

Always Powerful, Passionate and Provocative.

HARLEQUIN Blaze

COMING NEXT MONTH

Available March 30, 2010

www.eHarlequin.com

HBCNMBPA0310